CONFIDENT
Sensuality

A. VAN-DE-CRUIZE

Copyright © 2021 A. Van-De-Cruize
All rights reserved
First Edition

Fulton Books, Inc.
Meadville, PA

Published by Fulton Books 2021

Cover Photography by 100 Karat Photography

ISBN 978-1-64952-449-2 (paperback)
ISBN 978-1-64952-450-8 (digital)

Printed in the United States of America

Contents

Prologue 5
Chapter One 9
Chapter Two 16
Chapter Three 25
Chapter Four.. 38
Chapter Five... 61
Chapter Six 69
Chapter Seven 90
Chapter Eight 97
Chapter Nine 103
Chapter Ten 108
Chapter Eleven... 115
Chapter Twelve 128
Chapter Thirteen 139
Chapter Fourteen 166
Chapter Fifteen 189
Chapter Sixteen.. 200
Chapter Seventeen... 216

Prologue

"Melissa, honey?"

She can't be serious right now. But a girl can only hope. She does it again.

"Melissa!"

My name echoes through the cathedral ceilings and down the long hallways that make up our home.

"Come down here! I need a little help."

The panic in her voice makes her French accent sound even more French, and that should alarm the average fourteen-year-old girl. But I am not average. Nor is my mother, and since we're on a roll here, neither is my father.

For starters, tutors for three different languages, French, Italian, and Spanish, have frequented our home since I was five. I have learned the art of fencing, for crying out loud, and I have an English tutor for—*get this*—pronunciation, grammar, and vocabulary expansion. We can thank my over-the-top mother for that.

I realize I'm being repetitive, but we, my friends, are not an average family.

It'll do you some good to remember that.

"Melissa, I'm tired. Please."

Yes, Mother. So am I. I roll my eyes because her theatrics have always been her strongest trait. Not her best, but definitely her strongest.

"Melissa."

That time, my name held no panic, all business. I always found it interesting how my mother could switch into another emotion with pristine ease without a trace of evidence of the previous emotion.

So I answer, hoping that I at least sound tired. I mean, I don't sleep, and somehow instead of my eyelids getting heavier as the night carries on, they remain wired, almost as if they're preparing for the sun to rise. So here I am at 3:00 a.m. wide awake. "Yes, Mother."

"Come *here*." Yeah, she's definitely done panicking.

What on earth could possibly be so important that I have to be removed from my queen-size bed at three o'clock in the freaking morning?

I drag myself out of bed, nearly sliding off because of my satin sheets, and shuffle to the hall to follow the remnants of her persistent echoes.

The closer to the spiral stairs I get, the easier it is to hear our dog, Max, panting.

Except Max is snoring.

Therefore, Max is not panting.

Someone, as in a human, is actually panting. I'm thinking maybe it's because of the house's ability to make everything sound so pregnant with volume; maybe that's why it sounds like panting.

I slowly descend the first set of stairs toward said panting, and of course, the closer I get, the more noises my ears discover. *Was that something being dragged?*

I've made it to the second floor now (it's a three-story house), and I hear my mother say "Pass me the tape." She is likely speaking to my fourteen-year-old cousin, Ramona. My mother likes to call us fraternal twins, and every time she does, I roll my eyes. My cousin's parents, who also happened to be my aunt and uncle on my dad's side, died in a tragic accident when she was four, so she has been with us ever since. She too has endured the abundance of tutor glee.

I finally make it to the source of the array of sounds: the kitchen. My ever-so-helpful cousin is running the duct tape over to my mother, who is currently hovering over my very still father.

My father is incredibly still.

My father is not moving.

My English tutor always stressed the need to be specific in my writing. She would say, "And if you feel that you have difficulty with that, start by being more specific with your speaking. Add details, be more descriptive, and read more challenging books to enhance your vocabulary. Let it become second nature."

I do like English.

There is no steady rise and fall of his chest, no color or moisture to his originally voluminous reddish-brown lips. His smooth dark brown skin that contributed to my mocha complexion is now a dusky gray hue.

My mother, sporting red cheeks, looks up at me. Her usual blonde straightened bob is pulled into a short ponytail at the base of her skull. Her bright blue eyes are rimmed with red, and her hairline is decorated with beads of sweat. I gaze over at my cousin, and she is simply following my mother's line of vision.

I too am very still, since I refuse to add anymore clamor to the symphony taking place in this kitchen until someone offers me an explanation as to what is truly going on.

Chapter One

Seven Years Later

Melissa

Why am I even taking this suicide-inducing class? I shake my head, pushing a wayward curl out of my face as I approach my genetics lecture hall. Why didn't we ever have a science tutor? I hover outside the class waiting for Lacey, my stereotypically intelligent, Asian (specifically Korean) best friend to arrive so that we can sit next to each other like children.

Honestly, she is the reason I'm not failing miserably, granted I'm rather close, but that's not the point. The real reason I want to sit beside her is because when I don't fully follow the direction that the lecture is going in, which happens quite often, I'll glimpse over to her notes. I'll ask her questions and observe her interpretation, and that usually aids in decreasing my lack of understanding.

My professor doesn't appear to like me very much, nor does it seem that he has a great deal of patience where my understanding of this course is concerned. I'm certain of that because every time he catches me looking at Lacey's notes or conversing with her, he'll pause and make it a point to express his disapproval with his condescending stares or his stern disciplinary comments. Or he'll do that amazing thing where he'll put me on the spot, knowing I'm passing his class by the fine hairs on my chinny-chin-chin, and that the likelihood of me knowing the answer to anything he asks me is slim to none.

Initially, it made me uncomfortable. Well, I'm still uncomfortable, but now I find great pleasure in challenging his intense green-eyed unspoken threats.

As a matter of fact, while we await Lacey's notoriously late arrival, let's discuss just how intense Professor Angelo is.

He leaks sex.

I said it, and I meant it.

The man has no right to make me feel like a porn star every time he looks at me for more than a couple seconds at a time. It certainly doesn't help that he looks like an Adonis, with his curly dark brown hair, each lock moving in a direction of its own, olive skin, plump lips, and stupendously straight white teeth. Not that he smiles much.

He has a uniquely imperfect nose, and that simple fact makes him more real to me. It's slightly bent at the bridge, which I'm sure is evidence of a recent poorly healed fracture. Knowing the little that I do know about him, he probably refused to give the poor nose the appropriate amount of medical attention necessary.

Moving forward, he towers over my five-foot-seven frame at approximately six feet four inches. His voice—*my God*—his deep, raspy bedroom voice has each and every female in here sitting on the edge of her seat, praying for more recognition from him. *Any* recognition from him.

He doesn't particularly give any indication that he is aware of his Hollywood looks; however, let's say he is aware. Let's say he knows exactly what he does to women. It wouldn't make a difference because he's still one of the world's finest assholes.

I shake my head and purse my lips at his receding back, glimpsing into the classroom.

"Hey, hey," Lacey has finally graced me with her presence.

I glance down my wrist, peering at a watch, a watch that isn't actually on my wrist. I don't own watches. "What's this? You're on time?" I finally glance at the time on my phone.

She smirks. Lacey, in all her Asian-ness, has swag that emanates from her pores. She's gay, and she owns that part of herself, rather proudly, might I add, but only to the public eye. However, never in front of her family. They're all rather old-school Asian, so it is highly likely that they won't stand for her identification of sexuality. I always tell her she can't live like this forever, hiding who she is from her family. She doesn't like to discuss it for too long. She has long dark hair with blond tips and a lean physique, and her best features, I always tell her, are her hazel eyes and her lips. They're a lot more plush than the rest of her family's.

I always joke with her and tell her that her mom must have had a fair share of friends in her day. She looks nothing like her father.

Shrugging, she starts, "Not sure I'm interested in another one of Angelo's stares of disapproval."

I put on my best shocked face. "What? You mean you don't like it when he peers into the deepest darkest depths of your soul?"

She rolls her eyes. "All right, Shakespeare."

We stroll into the room of doom together.

Angelo slides his black-rimmed glasses off his face in a casual manner and simply says, "Good morning, Ms. Santino." That would be me. "Ms. Kim." And that's Lacey. Lacey Kim.

Pause.

So that greeting would have been normal had he looked at Lacey when he said her name. But he didn't. Instead he looked at me for the entire duration of time it took for him to address us both.

"Mornin'," Lacey mumbles. Oblivious. Uninterested. Unbothered.

I know we've been over this already, but chills never cease to run down my spine every time he says my name. However, like I said, I have to challenge him, so I stare back. "Angelo."

"*Professor.* Professor Angelo," he corrects me.

I snap my fingers. "Oh yeah. That's right. Forgot you were the professor for a second." Yes, I am being sarcastic. Yes, I am enjoying it. And yes, I do this very often to the Adonis professor.

Lacey chuckles. "You're pushin' it."

I shrug. "I'm not quite tired of the way he peers into my soul." He's disconcerting, yes, but somehow alluring.

"Weird ass."

I laugh a little too loud. "We've known this."

We take our seats, and class begins with genotypes and phenotypes. And of course, Angelo asks me the first question. I fight the urge to roll my eyes.

"Melissa, if you could get us started by explaining the difference between genotypes and phenotypes for the class, that'd be stellar. Thanks."

I glimpse at Lacey, but it appears that she too is enjoying this travesty. Shaking my head at the traitor that is my friend, I answer confidently. And what does Angelo say?

"Wrong."

Of course. "How?" I try not to put much disappointment in my voice, but if I'm going to judge my success by the smug look on Angelo's face, I'd conclude that a failure is on my horizon.

"Well, for starters, you seem a bit uncertain. You've defined one as the other. Even with that being said, I asked for the difference. You merely defined them incorrectly."

I straight-faced him. Ass. "Well, if you could just go right ahead and correct me for the benefit of a better education, that'd be stellar. Thanks."

It's awfully quiet in here. Side conversations and the pointless chatter that contributed to the constant background hum of the lecture hall has now come to an end. Angelo smirks ever so slightly, nodding as if admitting defeat, but I can assure you, there will be more. This is simply Angelo tipping his hypothetical hat off to me.

"All right, class…" And lecture begins, leaving me feeling just a tad bit on the edge of my seat, like all these other attention-starved women in this God-forsaken class.

Chapter Two

Melissa

In these last few minutes of class, I start gathering my belongings, not bothering at all about potentially missing important content because I don't understand a damn thing that's being transcribed anyways. I'll be paying Lacey in beer and pizza later to basically reteach the entirety of this lecture. At the official end of class, I'm pitching my offer to Lacey when Angelo calls my name. *I knew it. I knew there'd be more.* Lacey gives me a knowing smirk, nodding her head toward the door, signifying where she'd be waiting.

Everyone is filing out, drooling over the elusive Angelo. Meanwhile, I'm once again fighting one of my frequent urges to roll my eyes. "What's up?"

"I fear that you're failing my course, and not only that, but you don't seem to be taking it very seriously."

"I'm not failing. I'm *almost* failing. I think almost failing is proof that I care enough to not *actually* be failing."

He smirks, shaking his head. "I'm not sure that's the kind of attitude that will help you pass."

"I beg to differ. I'm not failing, Angelo. So on the contrary, this attitude is currently keeping me afloat."

"Melissa, you're only half a point away from failing. There aren't very many assignments left. You don't have any wiggle room, meaning—"

"I know what that means."

"These last couple of assignments," he continues, as if I never cut him off, "and the final are all you have. You cannot afford to do poorly on anything from this point."

"Wow. No pressure."

"On the contrary, Melissa, there is an immense amount of pressure where your final grade is concerned." He picks up his stupid briefcase. "Take heed."

Great. I've been dismissed.

"What was that?" Lacey asks, practically inhaling a cinnamon roll from the vending machine.

"He just kindly wanted to reiterate how poorly I was doing and maybe sprinkle a little judgment on me. No biggie."

She laughs. "As if you didn't already know. You're shit at this class."

"Wow. Your support is one of a kind."

She shrugs. "Since we're all stating the obvious…" Lacey trails off. I follow her line of vision to the bohemian full-bodied sophomore, Candace, Lacey's crush. Or obsession.

"Are you going to go speak to with her or…" I ask slowly, dragging my words for the sole purpose of being annoying.

"What?" she asks, distracted. "Oh yeah. I'm going over there." She stands right next to me.

"Right, so the only way to move is to, uh, move."

"Fuck you."

I laugh. "I'm serious. Just go." I nudge her shoulder with mine. Despite her initial trepidation, her swag remains intact as she saunters over to the brown-skinned beauty.

I stand there watching the interaction when my ass vibrates. Not even looking yet, I know it's my mother. However, I will say I'm surprised. She usually calls at very inappropriate times. The last time she called, it was 3:30 a.m.

"Mother, how are you?" My voice remains even since it doesn't take much for her to assume the worst.

"Busy, honey. Ramona has all these award ceremonies coming up, and her graduation is right around the corner."

Ah yes. Ramona. My cousin is graduating early because she's an unbelievable overachiever. Meanwhile, I can't get my genetics professor out of my ass about almost failing. "That's right!" I feign interest. "When is her graduation again?" A conversation with my mother is never complete unless we discuss my cousin's accomplishments.

"Oh, she's right here. Why don't you just speak to her?"

I hate when she does this. "Not right now, Mother. I have to study for—"

"Just hang on for a second, Melissa."

I throw a silent temper tantrum. There's some shuffling about sounds on the phone, and my patience with my mother immediately wears thin. "*Mother.*"

"Nope. It's Ramona."

Great, now I have to force a painful conversation with the bitch that is my cousin. "Hi, Ramona."

"Melissa."

I roll my eyes. "How is everything back home?" I'm at Brown University in Rhode Island, and she's back home preparing to graduate from—wait for it—Harvard fucking University. Massachusetts is home for me, so I'm only a little over an hour away from them. I hardly ever go back.

"It's great." She always sounds so nice and sweet and smug.

"Well, that's nice."

And now we sit on the phone in pure silence because we do not like one another. It's that simple.

Ramona is a beautiful, smooth dark black. She has never had a blemish, not a single flaw on her skin. Her eyes are dark but nicely almond-shaped. Her hair has always been thick and voluminous. And even though she was always more plump, she carried her weight well.

"I'm putting Mom back on the phone." She calls my mother Mom. She's my cousin. She should be calling her Aunt Lisa. Why am I so bitter about this, you ask? Because Ramona is a bitch, just in case I haven't mentioned it. I refuse to even pretend that we shared a womb.

"Great."

More shuffling noises. "Melissa, honey, will you be able to make it to her graduation? She has to know how many tickets to request."

Not a chance in the pit of hell. "I'll have to see what I have going on that weekend." Nothing. I have nothing going on.

We talk about Ramona's accomplishments once more, the weather, her busy life as a real estate agent, and then finally, my nonexistent sex life.

"Are you dating yet?" I've had one boyfriend my entire life. We broke up a year ago, and you would have thought he and my mother broke up.

"No, Mother. Not dating."

She sighs. Her theatrics were always overabundant. "Well, what's the problem? You need to show Roderick" (my ex) "that you've moved on."

"I'm not sure I do. As a matter of fact, I don't care what Roderick thinks." That's the honest-to-God truth.

"Honey, don't be silly. It's not about caring." I swear sometimes my own mother's theories are as difficult to understand as my genetics course. "These games are never-ending," she continues. "No matter what, you must always come out on top. You're gorgeous, for crying out loud. Why aren't you dating?"

I'm over this conversation. "Not quite sure. Are *you* dating?" I don't care, but she clearly wants to talk about dating.

"Yes, and, honey, he is sex on a stick."

I nearly gag. This conversation needs to end. "Mom, I have to go."

"Really? We just got on the phone."

No, but you just said sex on a stick. "Yep, gotta go. I'll call you later."

She sighs, "All right, honey."

We hang up, and I glimpse back over at where I left Lacey. She's still there working her charm, eliciting a smile from the bohemian goddess.

So I guess I'll just find a corner and continue to contemplate life.

I wander outside to a nearby courtyard and pull out the shit-tastic notes I took in lecture today. Despite the fall breeze, the sun's beams are spectacular, making it rather noticeable when a shadow obstructs its bright rays. I look up, and it's none other than Professor Angelo. This time I do roll my eyes because Jesus. "Can I help you, Angelo?"

"*Professor* Angelo."

I shrug. "Details."

He picks up my notes and peers at them through squinted eyes and furrowed brows. "Melissa, these notes are disgraceful." His voice, like I said, is like an orgasm for the eardrums, but it holds no emotion. Ever.

I laugh.

He doesn't think it's funny.

"They do suck," I concede. "But at least I took notes." That is a very poor point, but for dramatic effect, I snatch the note papers out of his hand.

"Right," he says, looking directly into my soul. "And I suppose that these are the notes that will save you? From failing my class, that is."

"Well, not *these* notes specifically." I am clearly not taking his concern seriously. He doesn't seem to like that very much. The thought elicits another laugh from the base of my throat, making this one just a little deeper than the last.

"Melissa." His tone is carrying the weight of disdain, and I do not like that, so I don't let him finish his thought.

"Why do you care so much?" I ask.

"Excuse me."

"You heard me."

"What kind of question is that?"

"One that you seem to be having a hard time answering."

"You're one of my students, Melissa. Why wouldn't I want you to succeed?"

I purse my lips. "Angelo, I know I'm not the only one doing poorly in your class. It's science, for Christ's sake. America's least favorite subject. Why is it that I seem to be the only one getting all these little special meetings about my almost failing grade?"

"Guess who has a date Friday night, bitch!" That would be Lacey, perfectly interrupting my near breakthrough with the Adonis that stands before me. "Oh shit." That would be her recognizing exactly what I just narrated. I shake my head.

I lean forward, not too far where this looks suspicious, but close enough so only he can hear. "Saved by the bell, Professor Angelo."

He smiles, and *fuck me*, it's replacing the sun rays. "Until next time, Melissa." He walks away.

"That is one perfectly sculpted ass," Lacey whispers.

I laugh. "Why are you whispering?"

She shrugs. "I don't know. I saw you and Angelo doing it."

My laughter only gets louder, attracting prying eyes. "So about this date…"

We discuss her pending date and the fact that my pending failure is dependent on how good of a teacher she can be over the next few weeks of class.

Chapter Three

Melissa

At some point during Lacey's tutoring session and my consumption of pepperoni pizza, my eyelids took over, and I fell asleep. I woke up with pizza sauce and cheese in my fingernails, my face plastered to the plastic pages of my textbook, and drool that traveled from the corner of my mouth to the corner of my eye. Fantastic. Lacey looks just as comfortable with her notes from several classes sprawled about her. The crazy thing is, I don't usually need to study. I'm a smart kid, if I do say so myself. My mother had a strange obsession with my and my cousin's education, but then there was science, my Achilles heel, my kryptonite. Give me a literature paper to write, a sonnet to analyze, or a mathematics equation to pick a part.

I wipe the drool of my face and kick Lacey's foot with the intent to awaken her, but she snores louder. Perfect. I stare at my new and improved notes and then at the textbook, and then my eyes connect with my Kindle. The Kindle wins. Shrugging, I concede that I will probably almost pass my genetics final, and I'm completely fine with that.

I've grown rather close to my book boyfriends because the real ones tend to disappoint. Lacey sides with my mother on my current dating status; she says the combination of my big curly hair, my bodacious curves, and smooth mocha skin should be enough for me to have multiple boyfriends. Except, where you have quantity, you typically lack quality. Don't get me wrong, I'm happy with my features, but with said features comes a lot of piece-of-shit men who see just that, features. Nothing more, nothing less. Long story short, get a Kindle.

*****

Yet another genetics lecture. Correction: yet another confusing and therefore unproductive genetics lecture.

"Melissa." There isn't a single class that transpires without Angelo picking on me to answer another question that I barely know the answer to. And by barely, I mean I do not ever know the answer. So here we go.

"Angelo," I answer.

"*Professor* Angelo."

"Semantics."

He shakes his head. "Students often confuse the two processes: meiosis and mitosis. There are a couple of factors that one can use to tell them apart and to further understand the cell division process."

"Right." *Please don't ask me to—*

"Would you please tell us what some of those differences are?"

"Sure." The silence in here is suddenly deafening. Someone drops a pencil, and someone else clears their throat. However, the most noise is coming from all of Angelo's unspoken words. His doubt is palpable, but it's quite evident at this point that I will not be answering this question correctly, which means I have to do something to distract us. Him.

"Angelo."

He rolls his eyes. "Answer the question, Melissa."

"In every class, you find a way to incorporate me into your lesson."

"I would hope that it is resulting in a bit more of your devotion to the content."

I shrug a shoulder. "Maybe, but it may also be resulting in a few of your other students feeling a sense of neglect."

"Then I would *also* hope that they, those who you claim feel neglected, would come to me to express that concern."

I glance at the clock, seven minutes until the end of class. "Me too, because I am feeling mighty special. It would be a shame though for everyone else to then, as a result, feel not so special."

Try as I might, this man doesn't look the slightest bit uncomfortable. As a matter of fact, he walks to the front of his desk, leans his beautiful ass onto it, and crosses his arms. It's almost as if he's goading me on.

Fine. I press on, "Some people simply do not find comfort in expressing what is often misconstrued as a rather juvenile concern."

"There is very little that I can do about someone else's self-esteem."

"Self-esteem? That's not what this is about, Angelo."

"No?"

"No."

"Enlighten us, Melissa."

"Am I the only one whose attention you're concerned about?"

"You seem to be the only one who is not paying attention."

The class chuckles. I roll my eyes, but I still take the bait. "I think you have what some might call a crush."

"Wow! Look at the time!" Lacey slams her textbook on her desk and begins to dismiss the class herself. Angelo hasn't moved, and neither have I, but there is an abundance of movement around us. "Come on! Let's go. Hey, pigtails! Move." She chucks her thumb in the direction of the door. I try to suppress my laughter, which ultimately just results in me smirking at Angelo.

"All right, class," he begins as people continue to follow Lacey's rather aggressive demands. "Be sure to follow up on today's material with the assigned readings." As the room empties, he finally graces me with one of his own smirks. However, his holds a wealth more of mystery than mine. The class eventually disperses, but not without a mixture of inquiring comments.

Angelo turns his attention to Lacey. "I'm going to have to ask you to kindly allow me to be the one to dismiss my class next time."

Lacey shrugs, exhibiting her nonchalant personality. "I don't know. I'm pretty dope at this."

Angelo shakes his head and asks her to step out as he'd like to exchange a few pertinent words with me. If we're being honest, I'm looking forward to it.

The door finally closes behind Lacey, and I'm waiting for the beratement, perhaps a little bit of judgement, and maybe just a dab of disapproval. He grabs a chair and places it directly in front of where I'm sitting.

So it's that serious? I roll my eyes. "Angelo, I doubt anyone took it seriously. Everyone knows you don't have a crush on me. I—"

"Your father owned a construction business, correct?"

Let's pause for a hot second here, guys. I'm not sure if I ever disclosed this, but English Literature has always been a subject of adoration for me. I love the idea of giving life to words. I live for the opportunity to taste the potential of each word before it leaves my mouth. Adjectives can either make me seethe or grant me great pleasure, but this time? My literary tongue does not salivate at the chance to grace this situation with descriptive words. Instead, I succumb to the vocabulary of an ordinary elementary school pupil. I was never an ordinary pupil.

Moving forward. "What do you mean?" I found words. I'm not very happy with them, but they've managed to work their way through the lump rising in the base of my throat.

"That is not a very concrete response, Melissa."

"You asked me a very nonconcrete question."

"That's not true."

I stare at him.

"I find it very interesting that you can often pull wit from thin air and engage in banter like it's your first language."

My voice somehow manages to elevate just above a whisper. "Thank you." But my thoughts echo throughout my skull, bouncing sound waves that create the words "What the fuck?"

"However, it seems that your ability to do so has suddenly been crippled."

I've never discussed my father with anyone, not even Lacey, which means Angelo either knows very little and possesses high hopes that his vagueness will prompt the release of further information, or he knows an abundance, and this is simply a test. I was never any good at his tests. If it is the latter, then his ocean runs deeper than I gave him credit for. "How do you know anything about my father?"

"Melissa, you haven't answered my question." That is a statement that makes it quite clear that he will not be answering any of my questions this fine morning.

There was always a profound sense of mystery about Angelo. His aura speaks volumes, and his presence beckons the damn angels. Or demons. Either way, it is apparent that Angelo is no ordinary man. However, I am no ordinary woman.

Okay, so he knows my father. Fine. I was shocked, but time is money. He asked me a question, and I'll give him an answer. "He did."

He nods. "Are you aware of the revenue that a construction company acquires?"

"Well, seeing as how my father owned a construction company," I pause for dramatic effect, "that seems to be something I would be aware of, Angelo. So in short, yes. Yes, I am aware of said revenue."

"There it is. That charming wit."

I shrug. "I try."

My phone buzzes, and his eyes gaze at the illuminated screen. "Would you like to get that?"

I furrow my brows as I'm sure he's aware of my current state of bewilderment. "What do you want, Angelo? Because I'm not sure if you've noticed, but there aren't very many connections between genetics and my father's old business revenue."

My phone buzzes again, eliminating the reflection of Angelo's prying eyes. I glance at the screen, expecting to be met with Lacey's impatience, but instead, it's my mother.

Angelo prompts me again to speak with my mother as he has plenty of time to chat. I squint my eyes at him, hoping that my display of both annoyance and impatience are simultaneous.

I send my mother to voicemail.

"Well, that wasn't very nice."

"Now is not the time for that witty banter you love so much. Tell me what you want."

"It's very simple. Someone has to pay the debt that your father accumulated with my family over the years." His tone carries the weight of boredom.

"Is that it? You want money?"

"No, I want your *father's* money."

"Well, I'm not sure if you heard, but, uh, he's dead. Been dead for a long time, Angelo." I shrug, but I also flinch. And I am certain he noticed.

"Melissa, you are a scintillating individual."

"Yes, I am." If I do say so myself.

"Which is why I am unsure as to why you are making this conversation so difficult."

"Well, if you'd stop engaging in all these damn word games…"

He removes his glasses in a casual manner, pulls a handkerchief out of his jacket pocket, and cleans his glasses. He then puts them back on his face and calmly states, "Money never dies."

I lean forward, place my elbow on my knees, and plant my chin into my palm. "Everything and everyone dies. Nothing lasts forever. Everything has an end." I sit back. "This conversation, however, seems to be living long and prospering."

"You and your mother seem to have an interesting and somewhat strained relationship—"

"I—"

"However, I'm sure you'd still hate to see any harm come to her."

My mother is a strange woman, and we do have an interesting, to say the least, relationship. However, I do love her, and that goes without saying, so yes, I would hate to see any harm come to my mother, but I refuse to show Angelo any emotion. Well, any more than what I've already shown. "Angelo, I have a genetics final to study for. I have papers due, and I don't know where this discussion is going. If we're going to continue to be frank, then I'd like to just address the fact that you've wasted a great deal of my time with this little game that I am sure you have worked hard to put together, but I just don't have it in me to play anymore." I begin gathering my things off my desk and shoving them into my backpack.

He stands the same time I do and steps just a hair closer. That step made all the difference because now we're exchanging one another's breaths. I could step back, but somehow, that to me is the equivalent to backing down, and that is simply not who I am.

"Whatever decision you make will affect everyone you love and care about."

"That sounds awfully similar to a threat."

He shrugs. "You can call it what you'd like, as long as you are aware of the meaning. Your father made his decisions. He's dead, and you're still being affected by them. The choice is now yours, but so is the consequence. That being said, I can ask your mother, or you can give me your word that you will pay me what is owed." Somehow, the term *ask* doesn't hold the same meaning when he uses it. He is promising that he will indeed do more than asking to get what he wants.

I glance at his lips just for a second. Then I meet his green eyes. "What exactly is owed?"

He smirks. "Half a million."

Jesus. "Half a million. Where do you suppose I get that from?"

"Well, if we're going to continue to be frank," he says, repeating my words to me, "I do not care."

I'd love more than anything in this moment to lash out and partake perhaps in a complete meltdown. I'd also absolutely love to give Angelo a piece of my mind, but my pride won't allow it. That again would be the equivalent to admitting defeat.

"Excuse me." I try to step around him, but he doesn't allow it.

"Do I have your word, Melissa?"

"Yes."

"Perfect. Have a good evening."

Fuck you. "You do the same, Angelo." I walk away with my chin up but with my spirits low. I am at least grateful that I still have my dignity because begging was becoming a strong consideration.

I can't even get the police involved. There isn't a chance in hell that they'd believe some young college kid with zero proof over a well-established professor. However, if we're being honest, as strange as this may seem, I feel that I am better than that; I am beyond calling the police. Getting the law involved, although it may appear to be the safer route, also feels like a cop-out, for lack of a better word, and therefore not so safe.

Granted, I still have not even the slightest clue what I am going to do about this particular circumstance that my father so kindly, and perhaps unknowingly, set up for me prior to his death, but so far, what I do know is that I have to dig a little deeper into his life and find out the connection between him and my family. I have a world's worth of questions that I am certain Angelo will not be answering for me. I also cannot ask my mother because her theatrics and poor emotional management skills will sink us deeper into the unknown.

Chapter Four

Angelo

Melissa is a brilliant woman. She will likely catch on to what my true intentions are prior to my execution, but at that point, it will no longer matter.

She will need an occupation because her pride will not grant her the permission to simply ask her mother for what I am asking of her. There is no legal occupation that will give her what she needs financially, or rather, what I need from her. Thus, her peace of mind, her sanity, and inevitably, her safety are all in the palm of my hand. I'm very satisfied with that knowledge due to the fact that her father, Ivan Baldeo, eliminated my family's peace of mind, sanity, and safety. I promised my dying father that I would attain justice for his death. I'm simply one step closer to doing so.

Mr. Baldeo was never a man of his word, and he was quite the selfish one at that. His temper was volatile, and he had a significant reputation with the law to show for it. However, he had money. As a matter of fact, he had wealth. Wealth lasts for decades and sometimes, if it is managed well, for centuries. So, yes, he is dead, but his wealth went on to live a long a prosperous life with his family. Well, primarily his now-widowed wife.

Melissa will learn sooner or later what she was born into. Again, at that point, all that I have set out to accomplish, as far as her family is concerned, will be complete.

I begin organizing my graded and ungraded students' assignments when my lab assistant, Stacey, comes in. "Hi, handsome."

She's thin with perfect white teeth, dark hair, ocean-blue eyes, high cheekbones, and full lips. She's very pretty, but there isn't much about her that makes me want to cross that student-professor line. She has, however, made her interest quite clear.

"Did you need me to do anything for you before I head out?"

I never do. "No. Thank you."

"Sure. So I sterilized all the equipment in the lab…"

I fight the urge to roll my eyes as she begins listing everything she did. All of which are parts of her job description. So I've already made the rightful assumption that her duties are complete.

Stacey has an impressive resume, but these unnecessary conversations that we have are truly exhausting. One would think that my open display of disinterest would be enough to deter the advances, but not her.

The classroom door swings open, and within its frame stands the witty Melissa and her sidekick, Lacey. "Yo, forgot my phone when I was dismissed," Lacey proclaims.

I wave my hand in the direction of where she sat to indicate that she's free to search. I look back over at Melissa, and she's leaning against the doorframe, smirking.

"Well, anyways," Stacey continues, completely disregarding our small audience. "It's Friday, and I've got nothing to do, so…" She shrugs and slides me her card. I would have rolled my eyes, but Melissa does it for the both of us. That appears to be a specialty of hers. Stacey makes her way out, and Lacey waves her phone at me.

"Congrats." I deadpan. "Keep better track of it next time."

"I'll do my darndest. Chances are low though, so don't hold your breath or anything." And with that, she's gone, sauntering past Melissa, who stays put at ease against my doorframe, likely to state the obvious about my dreadful encounter with Stacey.

"Seems you've gotten yourself a secret admirer," she starts.

"Not so secret," I clarify.

"She certainly thinks so."

"And you know what she's thinking?"

"Of course. I know what a lot of people are thinking."

"Please, do tell." I lean against my desk since that seems to be the tone of our conversation. My body language, I'm sure, still expresses its doubt in her words.

"Tell you what? What *I'm* thinking?"

"Of course not. I already know that."

"Right. Then I guess this conversation is over."

I shake my head, watching her walk away. Like I said, brilliant. I'm looking forward to what her future will reveal to her. Or us, rather.

Melissa

I'm on our living room floor with my laptop, textbook, and homework. Lacey and I share a pretty spacious two-bedroom off-campus apartment that my mother primarily funds. Except the only thing I've done as far as my homework is concerned is open my textbook. My laptop's purpose is to expose me to jobs.

"So you're just gonna pay him?" Lacey asks, tapping away at her keyboard, being an actual student. I filled her in. She thinks this whole thing is cool, assuming that my dad was some sort of mafia lord or something. But she's also Lacey, so she fancies those kinds of myths.

"What else do you suggest I do?"

"You can't just, like, lie to your mom or something and ask to borrow the money?"

"What kind of lie—"

"Yeah, you're right." She looks up from her keyboard to say "That *is* a lot of money to lie about." She shrugs. "Bruh, you might be doomed."

"Thank you, Lacey." I hope she senses the sarcasm in my tone.

She clasps her hands together loudly, causing me to startle a bit. "Dude, I never told you about my date." I roll my eyes, and not only because her attention span is sometimes as good as trash but because there are bigger fish to fry at the moment.

"Lacey, I have to find half a million bucks. I'd love to hear about your date, just maybe after I find at least one job."

"Or ten."

"What?"

She sets her laptop down. "Mel." She calls me Mel when she's attempting to be serious. "This doesn't add up."

I squint my eyes and furrow my brows. "So you're saying I need ten jobs?"

She rolls her eyes. "Did he give you a time frame for when all this cash needs to be in his hands?"

"No."

She squints. "And where does he expect you to get it from? Do you really believe that Angelo is expecting you to come up with all that money?"

"Well, yeah."

She purses her lips.

"I mean, don't get me wrong," I continue before she begins the pending beratement, "I knew that there was something that wasn't particularly concrete about this whole 'get me my money' situation. But I figured that I should probably dig into the history between him and my father first. Maybe find out why this money is so important or what specifically it's connected to."

"I don't think that it's even about the money. This whole thing definitely runs a little deeper than some petty cash. I think he's running game on you, kid."

I think back to my little discussion with Angelo, attempting to fit Lacey's concept of game-running into my mental investigation. My thoughts are running rampant, looking for an idea to settle on.

"Do you think it even has to do with my father, or was he just distracting me?" I shrug, still a little unsure of what exactly I'm trying to discover.

"Well, if you're distracted with being hung up on a sensitive topic such as your deceased father, then you can't really snatch him up on his bullshit, as in the real reason he wants you searching for the dough." Lacey is very intelligent, but the slang will never leave her soul.

"Exactly. Physical distraction is one thing. But emotional and mental distraction?"

"That'll fuck a bitch up mighty quick," she states, finishing my thought.

"That's what he wanted."

"That's what he got," Lacey confirms, pointing her finger at me. She tosses a chip into her mouth. Where did that even come from?

"Not for long." I decide.

She furrows her brows. "Explain."

"He's expecting me to begin the quest to attain said money."

"Correct."

"And like you mentioned, he doesn't think that I can. It's just a mere distraction, tes?"

"Yes."

"But I will anyways."

She tilts her head. "Come again?"

I set my laptop down and stand to my feet. "Hear me out." I wave my hands about, dismissing her confusion. "I'll get a job, but I'll also ask my mom to borrow a significantly lesser amount. And I'll give that to him, sort of as a down payment." I stare at her, awaiting some sort of acknowledgment, but when I don't get one, I proceed. "I'll just have to put on a show. Make him feel like his plan is going accordingly."

"Okay. Then what?"

"Lacey." I kneel in front of her. "He wants to play, so I'll play."

"But, Melissa, something tells me Angelo's been playing for quite some time now. He knows this game very well. He can probably play circles around you. Are you sure you don't just wanna call him out on his bullshit and see what he does?"

I lean back on my heels. "Something tells me that that way won't reap the outcome that we'd like it to either. If I end this game too soon" (I use my finger for air quotes around the word *game*), "I may be starting a war."

She nods, but we're both unsure of how this will pan out. The only thing I'm sure of is my next step. I have to call my mother.

Fantastic.

"Can I tell you about my date now?" she asks again, separating me from sinking deeper into my thoughts.

"I suppose I don't have a choice."

She shrugs and then begins telling me about her date.

I continue my job search.

Apparently, Candace, her date, is a jack of all trades with an interest in art, but her major is in forensic science. Her ethnic background is African and Caribbean, and she has the softest lips ever. Lacey is obviously excited, while I pray to the heavens that I can get hired somewhere within the next twenty-four hours.

"So are you guys going on another date or…?" I finally ask.

"Yeah. She's cool." She shrugs as if it's no big deal.

"Right. You just spent half an hour talking about your date with her because she's cool," I repeat, mocking her dismissive shrug.

She squints her eyes at me. "Don't start."

I shrug for real this time. "I'm just saying…"

"*Okay*. Conversation over." Lacey doesn't like discussing her feelings, but for the record, she has liked Candace for a while now. I've always called it a crush, but only because Lacey is not, in any way, in tuned with her emotions. Calling it a crush is an easier alternative for Lacey's lack of emotional intelligence than just accepting what is taking place between the two of them.

"How's the job search?" she asks, completely averting the direction this conversation has taken.

"Amazing."

"Really?"

"No."

She laughs. "Why don't you try interning somewhere? Like in a lab or something. Anything science-related, typically pays well."

"Interns are not paid, are they?"

"They can be. Just depends on how you filter your search and which job search platform you're using."

We go through a number of different ways to tailor my search for better results. By the end of the night, I've applied to three forensic labs, one of which Candace works at according to Lacey; seven coffee shops, all of which pay minimum wage; and two front desk secretary positions. I'm hoping I can pair one of the higher paying jobs with one of the coffee shop ones so that a solid consistent income is guaranteed. Winter break is approaching, and we've already established my lackluster desire to visit home, so it looks like I'll be a working woman. On the bright side, my major is undeclared, so perhaps working in one of these facilities, not particularly including the coffee shop, could help me figure out what I'm doing with my life.

"I need a plan," I declare.

"What you mean? Like a new plan?" She nods. "I agree because that first one is pretty shitty, Mel." She shakes her head. "You can't play games with the man who invented the games."

"I meant for my mother. Like what am I going to tell her to get this money borrowed?"

"Oh. Huh. Well..." She taps her chin rhythmically.

I roll my eyes.

"Tell her you need to get your car fixed."

"Nah, we have a warranty on it. My deductible is only a hundred bucks, and that jeep is pretty new. There shouldn't be anything wrong with it that's that expensive to fix."

"Damn." We're both silent for a minute, mulling over our very few potential options. "Wait a minute. How much are you even asking for?"

"Ah yes. I suppose a number will help us come up with a fitting story. Two thousand?"

"That's it?"

"Anything more will make it harder to come up with a lie."

"Well, we need to think harder, Mel, because that does not seem like a convincing enough amount for Sir Mafia Lord Angelo."

I roll my eyes. "Where am I supposed to get the rest from?"

"You have a nice ass. I'm sure a few of these night clubs could use a chocolate dancer."

I fling the couch cushion at her. "I'm serious."

She dodges the pillow and shrugs, as if to say "'Tis a lost cause, kid."

"I just want to give him something. I don't really think that the amount matters."

She shrugs again. "Suit yourself, but if that's all you're gonna give him, then you need a plan beyond the one you have now."

"You mean like a follow-up?"

"Sure, a follow-up," she repeats.

I need to keep him on his toes. I cannot let him know what I think I know.

*****

I went to bed with a plan, and I woke up with the weight of the world on my eyelids.

Today is the day.

It feels like judgment day since it's the day Angelo will likely judge me for failing this Biology final miserably. That's exactly what will happen.

I am going to fail, just so we're clear.

Lacey and I did study. After our rigorous job search and master planning, we actually studied. However, a final is just that. The conclusive end of a series of smaller exams. The final opportunity to save my ass. Therefore, everything that has taken place prior to this moment inevitably does not matter. The booklet of information that was slapped in front of me by the beautiful asshole that stands before me, Angelo, is the only thing that will seal my fate.

Before I even made it to my seat, I almost didn't. Allow me to explain. I wanted to stop for coffee at one of the on-campus barista carts. Lacey kindly informed me that that will result in my tardiness to the final exam. Her exact words were "Coffee? You wanna get coffee *now*?" She stared at me.

I shrugged a shoulder.

"Bitch," she continues, "they take years to make one coffee." Shaking her head, she states, "Angelo is going to make a spectacle of you."

I shrugged again with both shoulders with my palms turned upward. "Angelo will make a spectacle of me with or without this coffee."

"You might be right, but today may not be the day to test that theory, especially with everything else going on. You don't want to try to get in his good graces?"

I shake my head, slightly defeated. "That ship has sailed."

She shrugged. "That too may be a fact. On that note, I'll see you in there."

I got my coffee after what felt exactly like ages and ambled to the science building down the hall toward my exam to meet with doom. Except Angelo interceded, reminding me that "your seat and the exam are both inside the classroom."

Instead of apologizing and taking heed to Lacey's wise advice with getting in his good graces, I chose this moment (of all moments) to do the complete opposite.

"What gave you the impression that I was unsure of where both my seat and my exam are located?"

He shrugs. "Your apparent tardiness, your blatant disrespect for this course, and your obvious disdain for your success. Those are just a few things."

This part. This part right here is where I seemed to have forgotten where my fate lies. Observe.

I took a step toward him. A step filled with an abundance of intent. Intent that you will soon see goes unnoticed. Or ignored. It truly just depends on how you apply your perspective.

"I just wanted coffee, honey. If you wanted some, all you had to do was ask."

He smirks, but just barely. Quite frankly, I only noticed because of how much space I had eliminated between the two of us. However, he says nothing. Therefore, I sip my coffee, bless him with one of my world-renowned smirks, and continue my amble into the classroom.

CONFIDENT SENSUALITY

Now I stare ahead, even with the exam beneath my nose, praying to the heavens that the pending conversation with my mother will go better than this exam. I look over at Lacey, I look up at Angelo, and then I look at my exam.

Here we go.

*****

People are filing out of the classroom one by one. I can just smell the scent of nerdy success and perspiration, my perspiration. Looking at the final question, I shade in my response and close the devil's booklet.

Lacey was finished a solid twenty minutes ago. I get up and drop my finished exam in front of Angelo on top of his desk, and I saunter out, hopefully looking better that I feel.

I stand just outside the classroom looking for Lacey. I wasn't expecting her to be far, and of course, she is cuddled up in a corner, pouring on the charm with the one and only Candace. I shake my head. Candace doesn't stand a chance.

Welp, I guess I'll call my mother. I turn on my heels, planning to head back to our apartment to start brainstorming lies for dear old mommy when I feel someone's cool calloused hands on my wrist.

"Melissa."

What in the actual fuck? I turn to face the familiar voice. "Roderick?"

"Hey, I uh…My little sister goes here, and," he clears his throat, "I was just stopping by for she and I to have lunch together."

Okay, and? "That's great. I don't really see her around much." She's short and kind of frumpy, but she has the sweetest honey brown eyes and the cutest round face. They're family is Hispanic, but he has a darker complexion than his little sister, so people don't often assume that they're family when they're together. They have always been close though.

"Ah, she's a fashion major, so it's probably not likely for the two of you to run in the same circles."

Hmph. Right. Fashion and science don't even share a spectrum. So you came looking for me. The fact that you knew exactly where to come, however, means you've been speaking to my mother. Fantastic.

Moving forward, this particular bone will be picked exclusively with my dear mother. "So how have you been?" *Not that I give a rat's ass.*

"Pretty good. Grad school is kicking my ass." He gives a short laugh. "But other than that, I'm doing all right."

"Well, that's good."

He nods, and now we stand here awkwardly.

"Look, truth is, I was hoping I'd run into you."

I bet you were.

"I miss you, and I was hoping maybe you and I could grab coffee…"

I stare at him.

"And catch up a bit."

Hmph. If I recall correctly, he broke up with me, and I don't even remember why, which is even more of an indication that this whole "catch up over coffee" thing will be a complete waste of my time. I do not miss him. Time does this thing where it remains consistent no matter what. That being said, I depended on time to get over him. Now the sight of him only surprises me. There is no excitement, yearning, reminiscing, or desire. I'd like to say as much because I'm feeling rather empowered and immensely rebellious toward my mother. I want, more than anything in this moment, to know that he will be informing my mother of my wordy rejection. However, Angelo has plans of his own.

His hand briefly lands on the small of my back, but with that brief connection comes a swarm of electricity. I take a sharp breath and fight the urge to search our surroundings to see if anyone witnessed the forbidden action. Instead, my eyes find Roderick's. He most certainly witnessed the forbidden action, which makes me feel like Angelo knows exactly what he's doing, which also leads to the realization that Angelo is...jealous?

Right?

I mean why else would he feel the need to make such a brazen and intimate form of contact with a very sensitive part of my body? I guess it's not that sensitive, but it is intimate.

I take my eyes off Roderick and place it on Angelo, and I squint, expressing without words that I'm onto him, yet I'm also still a tad bit confused. He simply extends his hand and introduces himself to Roderick as Salvatore Angelo.

Wow. I am flabbergasted. First and last name. My eyes widen. I'm still looking at him.

Pause.

Here is my theory, guys: Angelo saw Roderick and I interacting, somehow felt a pang, so to speak, in his ego, and thought that perhaps coming over here and touching me with the knowledge that I will react will give Roderick the impression that there is history between he (Angelo) and I. Roderick will retreat, and Angelo wins.

Angelo, you clever man.

Except I am a woman of intellect. That feeling of empowerment has returned, so I interrupt their small talk by simply asking "Is there something you needed, Professor Angelo?"

He falters, ever so slightly, but he recovers rather quickly. With ease, he says, "Oh, I'm sorry, Melissa. Was I interrupting something important?"

I look down at my phone, pretending to check the time and specifically to avoid making eye contact, just so I can hold onto my bravado. "You were. Roderick and I were just trying to set up a time to have coffee." *Fuck. Fuck! Now I have to have meaningless coffee with Roderick. So much for rebelling against Mother dearest.*

"Coffee," he repeats, as if it's a foreign word.

"Yes. It's a caffeinated beverage." I almost laughed, because I mean, that was a great dig.

He nods. "Can I speak with you before you leave?"

For heaven's sake.

"What's happenin,' bitch?" Lacey's perfect timing interrupts our rather uncomfortable exchange.

Roderick looks confused, Angelo looks...well, I'm not sure, but he's looking at me. And Lacey looks unbothered.

"Bruh, what the fuck took you so long? You were in there for *years*." She looks at Angelo. "'Sup?" Then she looks at Roderick, squints, and sighs. "Seriously?" Boredom takes hold of her voice. Lacey has never been a fan of Roderick. She always said she thought I was settling. Despite my lack of tolerance for him now, I always felt like he had a solid plan and direction as far as where his life was headed. However, Lacey's arguments were always "It's not about that. It's that his emotional capacity will never match yours. You may not see it now, but in a few years, you'll see that your mental growth will have exceeded his."

"Good to see you, Lace."

"Lac-*ey*." She shakes her head. "And I can't say the same, Rod." She looks at me. "I'll be in a corner somewhere. Come find me when"—she waves her hands carelessly amid the three of us—"this is all done."

She saunters off.

Roderick, likely exhausted and/or finally uncomfortable with this encounter, offers to text me later with plans to meet up for some damn coffee.

CONFIDENT SENSUALITY

I will not be responding.

I watch him walk away and finally face Angelo. "What can I help you with?"

"I'm not sure you can help me, Melissa."

I roll my eyes. "Are you implying that I need your help?"

"I'm not sure I can help you either."

This has already gotten old. "What do you want?"

"You know what I want."

I try not to show my surprise and/or my panic. I'm assuming he's talking about the obscene amount of money my father so-called owed him. He couldn't have expected me to have come up with all of that money this soon. "You want that *now*?"

"I want proof."

"Proof of what?" I sigh with impatience at his lack of response. "Angelo, you need to use your words. This isn't a game."

He steps closer, and I notice his eyes turning a deeper shade of green. His nostrils flare, and his breath has a minty chocolate aroma. "At what point, did I insinuate that this was a game?"

What's this? Is he angry? Hmph. This is new. Angelo has a way of making his indifferent (for lack of a better word) demeanor seem charming. That demeanor of his is so effortless that this anger feels potent and a little misplaced. I shrug. "Well, I don't know, Angelo. You brought up things about my father that I knew nothing about. You then tell me to give you money, but you don't say when, and now you want proof of God only knows what. There are too many holes in your demands."

His breathing pattern has changed. It's almost like he's thinking about each breath before he allows the actual exchange of carbon dioxide and oxygen.

I tilt my head to create the illusion that I'm studying him, which I suppose I am, but only to find his weakness so I can play this game, so to speak, as effectively as he plays.

I'd like to touch him, but I'm not that brave. If I could just trace my finger over the stubble on his sharp jawline, or run my fingers through his hair, or maybe brush my lips against his…

"Professor Angelo." Stacy stands before us with a perplexed look on her face. However, her bright blue eyes hold a bit of mischief. She's perplexed, sure. But likely only because she now sees me as competition, whereas prior to this moment, she did not.

Chapter Five

Angelo

I'm grading each exam as they are handed to me; it makes no sense to allot a later time to do this very simple task.

Much to my surprise, Melissa passes her final exam. Don't get me wrong. It's not by a great deal, but a pass is a pass. I'm sure she'd appreciate this. It's a shame I have to hold it over her head.

Melissa is intelligent, but she's also dismissive. She likes to fabricate a facade using her wit, her charm, and sometimes her looks. This facade, however, is transparent and therefore ill-constructed. I'll have to expose just how transparent it is when we discuss what her options are as far as her final exam goes.

You're making this far too easy for me, Melissa.

I'm gathering exams and other necessary end-of-semester paperwork, preparing to leave in time to run into Melissa. I'm sure she hasn't made it far. She just finished her exam. As I'm stepping foot out of my classroom, I see Melissa interacting with a tall likely Hispanic individual. He's built. Not lean, but genuinely muscular. And he seems to have thick curly hair. He appears to be attractive, but not at all her type. However, she seems familiar with him. No shyness, novelty, or hesitation where her movements are concerned.

Allow me to explain. Growing up, I was forced to learn how to read people. Words and/or purposeful actions hold little to no meaning. Demeanors, gestures, unguarded moments—they speak volumes.

With that being said, both his awkward stance and shifty eye contact tell me he's unsure of himself despite his good looks. However, his uncertainty stems from something deeper than a mere lack of confidence. Melissa's demeanor is sure. She knows him, which means it would only make sense for him to know her. Except he's acting like this is their first encounter ever. It doesn't matter how long it has been since you have seen someone; familiarity is always evident. This time, it isn't, which means the consistency has been interfered with by an outsider. I'm going to take a wild guess and assume her mother had a little something to do with this encounter taking place before me.

I was hopeful that with this man's trepidation, this conversation would come to an abrupt end, especially with Melissa's lack of patience for bullshit. However, it seemed to just go on, with no purpose or end in sight, so I took it upon myself to introduce myself.

"Salvatore Angelo," I said, extending my right hand while placing my left hand on the small of Melissa's back, with the intent being to rescue her from a conversation that is clearly overdone.

The young dapper individual introduces himself as "Roderick Castillo. Pleasure to meet you." His handshake was firm, and there appears to be more bass in his voice with me than there was when he was conversing with Melissa.

I wonder why. All he needs to do now is stick his chest out and beat it with his fists. Ladies and gentlemen, a man should never feel the need to prove that he is a man, especially to another man. But if he wants to play and be embarrassed, so be it.

I have the sudden urge to trail my fingers up Melissa's spine, just to drive my point home, but she has plans of her own. "Is there something you needed, Professor Angelo?"

Ouch. She knows her conversation with Sir Roderick held just as much pleasure as my conversation with him. I don't why she chooses now to fight my attempt to rescue her. "Oh, I'm sorry, Melissa. Was I interrupting something important?" I make eye contact with her, daring her to continue with her stunt. And I just know she will.

"Yes. Roderick and I were just trying to set up a time to have coffee."

Fucking coffee with this *bitch?* "Coffee." What else can I say? She is wasting her time, and she knows that. Her level of intellect exceeds his by a long fuckin' shot.

"Yes, it's a caffeinated beverage." I almost shake my head at her attempt to make a dig at my intelligence with her never-ending sarcasm.

We're wasting time. I came out of my classroom with one purpose in mind: to remind Melissa of what is owed. However, with our one-man audience, I feel that now is the perfect time to turn up the charm a bit, ask her a question in a way that makes her believe I am giving her an option. Show Roderick here what it means to be a man when she approves my request, because she will. "Can I speak with you before you leave?"

"What's happenin,' bitch?" Lacey's perfect timing interrupts our rather uncomfortable exchange.

CONFIDENT SENSUALITY

Roderick looks confused, and Melissa is gazing at me, which somehow makes my balls twitch. And Lacey looks unbothered.

Lacey takes this time to berate Melissa and toss just a couple of insults Roderick's way, which is just perfect. If Lacey feels comfortable doing so, then I was correct: there is history here, and I'd like to know more about it.

Lacey makes an exit, and now Roderick announces that he will be contacting Melissa later about the fucking coffee.

I watch her and watch him walk away.

"What can I help you with?" she asks with little tolerance in her voice.

Fine. Back to business. "I'm not sure you can help me, Melissa."

She rolls her eyes, and that truly does strike a nerve. Every time she does it, sometimes it bothers me more than other days. Today's one of those "more than others" days. And there aren't very many things that can get under my skin.

She asks me if I'm implying that she needs my help.

I most certainly am. I'm just waiting for you to admit it so I can deny you. "I'm not sure I can help you either." What I don't always understand is her need to beat around the bush. She knows what I'm talking about.

"What do you want?"

"You know what I want."

I stare at her, watching the recognition set in. Her light bulb moment yields the words "You want that *now*?" The money, of course.

"I want proof."

"Proof of what?" She sighs. "Angelo, you need to use your words. This isn't a game."

A fucking game. She thinks that my obtaining justice for my father is a fucking game?

Easy, tiger. "At what point, did I insinuate that this was a game?"

She shrugs. I may just strangle this woman right here right now and speed this whole shitshow up. "Well, I don't know, Angelo," she starts. "You brought up things about my father that I knew nothing about. You then tell me to give you money, but you don't say when, and now you want proof of God only knows what. There are too many holes in your demands."

Of course, there are holes. Because exposing you to the truth too soon will cause everything that I worked for to crumble.

Because you're too fucking smart for your own good.

Because you're already too close to the truth.

Because when all is said and done, I still have to take your life. And I cannot let you see that coming because you won't let it happen. You don't realize just how powerful you are, just how strong you are, and when you find that out, Melissa, you will be unstoppable.

Because I'm a fucking coward, and I don't want to meet you when you tap into yourself.

"Professor Angelo." Stacy removes me from making a rather large mistake, but I'm certain that that will later come with a price—the price of inquisition.

"Stacy." I state her name because I don't want any sense of invitation in my voice to make her feel like she can begin her pending bout of inquisition now.

Except her focus is on Melissa.

Heaven help us.

Melissa extends her hand. "I don't believe we've officially met. Melissa Baldeo."

Stacy takes an additional few moments to finally extend her hand. "Stacy. Professor Angelo's assistant and friend."

Seriously.

Melissa doesn't take the bait. "That's sweet. How long have the two of you been friends?"

Stacy, taking her time to respond finally, says, "Long enough."

"Hmph. That's a long time."

Suddenly there's laughter escaping my chest.

Now Melissa is laughing.

Stacy is not.

This isn't going to end well.

Melissa is waging a war, and I think she knows.

Chapter Six

Melissa

I was never interested in games. However, I do know how to play. So if she's interested, then what kind of person would I be to deny her her desire?

"I'm satisfied that the two of you have now had the opportunity to meet one another, but I do have to excuse myself." Angelo, finally sobering up from his laugh, begins his retreat. Traitor.

"Listen," she starts once Angelo is no longer in earshot, "I don't know what you think you're doing, but—"

"What do you think I'm doing?"

She squints her eyes.

Oh no. I'm so scared.

"It's no secret that every girl in that classroom wants a piece of Angelo."

A piece? Seriously?

"Don't be stupid," she continues. "There's no way he'd ever go for someone like you."

"Yo! I'm leaving in like ten seconds, bruh." Lacey ambles closer. "How do you keep finding people to talk to?"

"Lacey, meet Stacy."

Lacey gives Stacy her signature nod.

Stacy hesitates, then proceeds to look her up and down, and finally says, "Pleased to meet you."

"Right. You're weird. I'm leaving."

"I'll be right behind you," I call after her. I look at Stacy. "It's interesting that you think that I'm not in his league."

"There's nothing interesting about it. I'm just trying to prevent you from setting yourself up."

"Oh, *that's* what this is. Okay. Well, in the future, before you go saving some poor, defenseless chick from heartbreak, keep in mind men that all men go after what they want. They're predictable. They form patterns. Angelo came out here to speak to me. You came over here to speak to Angelo."

"Okay…"

"Let's just see how often that pattern upholds."

I don't let her respond, although I'm certain that she may turn up the notch a bit with her advances toward Angelo, but games with her will hold little complexity compared to the games I'll be playing with Angelo.

"I have an idea," I tell Lacey when I catch up to her.

She rolls her eyes and, in her DJ Khaled voice, says, "Another one."

"I'm serious! And not a single word until I'm done."

She shrugs. "Shoot."

"Okay, so there were a few things I noticed back there—"

"Yeah, you talk too much."

"Hush." I continue, "I think Angelo may have a crush on me." I wince, awaiting her response, but there was nothing. "Hello?"

"Oh, permission to speak, Sergeant?"

"Bitch."

She laughs, but I do not. "Okay, okay." She sobers up. "For starters, uh, duh. Of course, he has a crush on you."

I lose my entire mind. "What?"

"More like he's attracted to you. The term *crush* seems a bit too juvenile for someone like Angelo. However, I'm not sure he's interested in you deeper than a physical level to be honest."

I shrug. "You may be right, but either way, that's half the battle."

She stops. "Half the battle?"

"Yes, so that brings us to my plan."

She shakes her head, already aware of where I am going with this.

"I think I can make him fall in love with me."

She stares at me.

"What? Look, we've already agreed that he's attracted to me. That part's covered. If he falls in love with me, then I can get out of this whole 'you owe me money' stunt."

She crosses her arms. "You've officially lost your shit."

I shrug. "I literally cannot think of another grand idea. Nothing. You know there's a lot at stake here." I stare at her, awaiting her seal of approval.

Well, more like her promise that she'll help me. "I'm running out of time, and I can't ask my mother because she'll ask too many questions. And I can't come up with that kind of money with a regular job. I can't. I don't know what else to do, but I have to do *something*."

She sighs and shakes her head. "How do you propose we do this, kid?"

"No freakin' clue."

"Where did this idea even come from?"

"Stacy."

"That weird-ass chick back there?" she asks, tossing her thumb over her shoulder. "She told you to do this? I knew her screws were slack, bruh. I knew it."

"No, no, no." I stop her, waving my hands dismissively. I try to catch her up on what she missed while she was snuggled up with Candace.

"First of all," she says, interrupting me, "fuck Roderick and his coffee."

"Wait. There's more," I continue, filling her in.

"Angelo? Jealous? Hmph."

"I know. That's what I said." We get to our apartment and fling our belongings on the couch, and finally, I tell her about Stacy.

"Stay away from that bitch. She is way too invested in her fantasy."

"Exactly. I mean the audacity." I shake my head.

*****

The day progresses, and she goes to her afternoon classes to take her finals. I study for my philosophy final, but the truth of the matter is I don't need to. School isn't difficult for me. Genetics is.

Science is. All things science. And Angelo, of course. So I call my mother. Because why not?

"Why was Roderick outside my genetics class mother?"

"Roderick? Oh wow! How is he?"

"Hmm. Well, he seemed a bit disappointed about my rejection."

"Your rejection."

That wasn't a question. It was a statement. A confirmation. No surprise, no feigning ignorance, no arguments. "Yup."

"What'd you reject, Melissa? His attempt at making amends?"

Pause.

I know you think you know where this is going, but I can assure you, you don't.

Moving forward.

"Yes," I answer.

"Why?" Please understand that there is no dramatic effect to her tone and zero additional sighs. She's being curt, because when she's angry, there is no room for the theatrics.

"I was not interested in making amends, Mother." My tone is nonchalant. I couldn't care less that she's vexed about her manipulative scheme being denied by me. And I want her to know.

"It's not about that, Melissa."

Here we go.

"You had an opportunity to show that man that you're better than him, that you've achieved more, and that the breakup did not break you. And you blew it."

I roll my eyes. "I haven't achieved more than him. He's in grad school. I'm still an undergrad. You're paying my rent, and I'm almost certain I just failed my genetics final."

I pause for dramatic effect.

"I'm not better than him, Mother, and that's simply because I'm not better than anyone. I'm fine with not playing this game that you insist on setting up. I do not want to play."

"It doesn't matter what you want. There are certain things you just need to know how to do."

I pull my phone away from my ear to stare at it. "Okay, Mother. I gotta go." I give up.

She hangs up without another word. Fantastic.

*****

Finals are over, and I have to wait three days to find out if I passed my genetics course. Lacey is packing to go home to see family for Christmas, and I'm getting dressed for my interview.

The plan is still to get a job so I can put on this facetious show that I'm gathering all my coins to pay Angelo. However, said plan now includes trying to make Angelo fall in love with me and excludes asking my mother for any money. How I'm going to do all of this, I have zero clue. Stalking may or may not be in consideration. Lacey has already given me the third degree and her humble opinion on the matter:

"For starters, genius, how are you going to get him to even want to be closer to you?" she asked.

"I don't know." I shrugged. "Social media?"

She stared at me. "So you think you can just use social media"—she pauses to pinch the bridge of her nose—"to get him to love you?"

I was planning on responding with a perfectly logical answer, something along the lines of social media being a good place to start, but she cut me off.

"What the fuck do you think this is? A Netflix original thriller?"

"No," I said slowly, dragging out the word. "Social media is the gateway to stalking 101."

"Hell. It's the gateway to hell." She sipped her coffee. "That's what you meant."

"What do you think I should do, wise-ass?"

"Glad you asked." She smirks. "The goal is to get more time in with him."

"Right."

"Well, that just became a lot harder seeing as how the semester is over."

My shoulders deflate. "Right."

"But let's face it. If you passed that final, you still didn't do well in his class, so it would still benefit you to go over the exam with him afterward. And I mean every single question that you got wrong. And I can assure you, you got quite a few wrong."

"Great. Thanks."

She shrugged.

"Lacey, that will annoy him. He will lose his patience, and boom, tutor session ends prematurely."

"Oh, ye of little faith, friend."

I squinted my eyes at her mischief.

"Listen." She sipped her coffee again. "He's not going to tell you no, one. Two, don't be annoying. You're smart. Stress what you do know. Three, we've already established that he's attracted to you. Wear something cute but subtle. Remember, this is a game. Every move requires careful thought before execution."

*****

"That's nice," Lacey now comments on my interview outfit.

I'm wearing her black pencil skirt that stops just at the knees and a white button-up shirt that's tucked into the pencil skirt, with my pearl studs, some lip gloss, mascara, and black business pumps. I'm going to throw on my blazer, and I'll be ready to go.

"Thanks."

"It's a pretty basic outfit, but your bangin' body makes it look hot."

"What? Wait, so it's too revealing?"

She shrugs. "I mean there's not much you can do about your hips and ass. Unless you wear a garbage bag."

I fill out her skirt a little more than she would. She has more of an athletic build. I'm definitely more slim-thick, if you would. "This is true."

"So which job is this interview for?"

"That internship. The forensics lab?"

"Ah, yes. Don't fuck up."

"Great pep talk."

She smirks. "It's what I do best."

I shake my head. "It's really not."

She laughs hysterically.

I grab my resume, purse, and phone. "Wish me luck like a normal person please."

"Don't fuck up please?"

I flip her the bird and go on my merry way.

I get to my destination, Rhode Island Bureau of Forensic Analysis. It's on the top floor of the Federal Bureau of Investigation headquarters. The elevators open to a rather open and marble floor plan. The reception desk sits several feet in front of the elevator doors. I step up to it with the right amount of confidence, introducing myself to two women, one platinum blonde and the other rocking her natural afro. Both exceptionally professional in attire and makeup. My confidence remains in tow until they point me to a waiting area of at least ten other desperate participants waiting for their interview. All of which simply look like science geeks.

Yes, you can look like a science geek. These young dapper individuals are certainly pulling off the look.

Time moves at the pace of molasses as each student gets called in, all of whom walk out with a level of confidence that I did not possess walking in here. I take this time to truly assess my surroundings.

People are walking around with suits, white lab coats, specimens, and gloves, using lingo that I am not familiar with at all. There are desks that seat multi-monitor computers and a steady hum of chatter.

There are quite a few sets of double doors that I'm certain leads to where all the magic happens, where all the specimens, samples, evidence, and all the testing takes place. I'm flooded with a rather complex feeling of both excitement and nerves. If I get this, it would be an awesome opportunity to learn. I mean to really learn. But then there's the simple fact that I know very little where this field is concerned. And by very little, I mean nothing.

I know nothing.

I see a familiar figure in my peripherals. When I turn my head to confirm my suspicion, I'm pleasantly surprised to see Candace walking toward me. She looks so nice in her white lab coat and business attire underneath. Lacey already informed me that she is a lab assistant here, but they still placed her with a mentor, giving her the opportunity to have more exposure.

CONFIDENT SENSUALITY

"Hey!" I stand to greet her with a hug.

"You look awesome! How do you feel?"

"Ugh, like shit."

She laughs. "Well, I can slide you a few tips. My interview was pretty straightforward, but they like to throw a few scenarios at you to see how"—she pauses, looking for the right word—"emotionally stable you are."

"Hmph. Okay, like what?"

"Like have you ever been raped?"

My head jerks back. "Uh, no."

"Sorry I know that was forward, but depending on who they place you with, that may be the majority of the kinds of cases you will be sitting in on. So if that hits too close to home, they'll pick up on it, and your chances of working here will immediately vanish."

I nod, expressing my understanding.

"Or if you'll be out in the field a lot, gathering evidence, they need to know how you'll respond to a corpse. Basically, they need to know that you can remove yourself emotionally from a situation. Do not get attached to the story that makes up the case or to the people. Be strong."

"Okay, okay. I can be strong." I say that more to myself than to her.

She pulls me in for another hug. "I gotta go, but good luck in there, love."

"Thank you." She's so warm; I don't think I can see her being emotionally removed.

"Melissa." My name is called by a voice that holds an unpleasant familiar ring to it. I look back to see the fiery Stacy in her Louis Vuitton shoes, her leather pencil skirt, and her fitted blouse all covered by a close-fitting lab coat that has her name engraved on it.

What the fuck?

Be nice, be nice, be nice.

"Stacy, what a pleasant surprise." *Good job.*

"Can't say the same." She turns her back to me. "Right this way."

"So you work here?"

"No. I just wear a lab coat and walk around."

Okay. I definitely walked into that one. "I meant what do you do here?"

"I work here."

Why are you so good at being a bitch?

"You can wait right in here." She stands in a doorway, pointing inside a generously spaced office.

"Did everyone else get interviewed in here or…?" This seems kind of over the top for an internship.

"Nope. He said something about your resume being impressive, and quite frankly, I find that hard to believe."

Hmph. Well, believe it, bitch.

I start to say thank you, but the door closes behind me after I've just barely made it into the office.

I shrug anyways because I'm in here and she's out there. I think it's fair that I get to be just a little smug.

Walking over to the floor to ceiling window, I take in Providence, Rhode Island. It's beautiful in general, but it is breathtaking from up here. When I gaze down at the day-to-day chaos, it makes the silence of this spacious office seem almost deafening. Maybe even eerie.

"Ms. Santino." My name bounces off this vast window and collides with my face.

I know that voice.

I am very familiar with that voice.

I've listened to it lecture me for the fifteen-week duration of my genetics course.

Slowly, I turn around to lock eyes with none other than Professor fuckin' Angelo.

Well, fuck me sideways and seven ways to Sunday. What an unpleasant surprise. I am trying with great effort—an exceptional amount of effort, likely an overabundant amount of effort—not to succumb to the slew of emotions that are taking ahold of every muscle fiber in my now aching body. Have I mentioned, by the way, how delicious he looks in his black perfectly tailored slacks and his crisp white button-up that is currently rolled up to the forearm? His tie has been loosened, and his hair looks like he's ran his fingers through it over a dozen times. I'm speechless and a little breathless that it takes an immense amount of effort to remember to close my mouth. Because it was open.

His appearance is such a contrasting difference from how he dressed for the duration of our course, which was in a more casual manner.

"Ms. Santino," he says again with that deceitful smirk. "What a pleasant surprise."

Bullshit. I wish I could say as much, but I guess it's important, at least at this point, that I stay or get on his good side. "Likewise," I utter.

"Please have a seat." He gestures to the chair that sits in front of his desk. "Let's get started, shall we?" He sets my resume in front of him.

This is crazy. Although, Stacy's attitude makes a lot more sense now. Her words play back in my head: "He said something about your resume being impressive." Angelo would have never said that out loud about my resume unless he was planting a seed. And come to think of it, I'm certain that all those other science intellects that I was waiting with have resumes that mine can't even hold a candle to.

I look at him, making eye contact, realizing that if I get this internship, every aspect of my life will be in the palm of Angelo's manly hands.

I'm damned if do, damned if I don't.

He has devised a plan of his own. Lacey's words ring in my ears: "Every move requires careful thought before execution."

"Why do you see yourself fit to work in such a demanding field?" he asks.

Typical interview question. I can answer this. Except I can't. Because I haven't been interested in forensics until today. *Dammit.* "Well," I start, with no plan of action in mind at all, "forensics has always fascinated me." *Way to be generic, Melissa.*

"Has it?" He doesn't believe me. Of course, he doesn't. He knows why I'm really here.

Okay, okay, okay. I can do this. "Of course, it does. Forensics is a science and an art. I guess I'm fascinated because science is usually pretty straightforward, but forensics offers the opportunity to use more outside-the-box thinking. There isn't necessarily a solid answer, and that's what draws me to it."

He leans in, folding his hands on his desk, asking "Can you be more specific?"

I'm on to you just as much as you're on to me, Angelo.

I lean forward, planting my palms on his desk. "I think I'm going to enjoy getting into the minds of the prosecuted." I shrug. "Learning their motives."

"Hmph. Very well." He shifts some papers around his desk. "Now, Melissa, I've had the pleasure of grading your exam."

Oh God. "And although you passed, it still was not a grade that would permit an internship here."

I stare at him, unaware of what he wants me to say exactly.

So he continues, "Would you say your grade is a reflection of your performance here if granted this opportunity?"

"Of course not. Learning theory activates a different part of the brain than learning in the field. I mean, I'm sure you knew this." I stop speaking to give him the chance to respond, but he's still just looking at me expectantly. Clearly, my rebuttal is not thorough enough, so I continue with, "Personally, if I can get my hands on whatever it is I'm learning about, things will make much more sense to me."

"Is that with all subjects? Or just science?"

I shrug. "Honestly? Just science." Makes no sense lying. I'm sure he already knows.

He shakes his head.

Pause.

I've been biting my sarcastic tongue, because he and I both know how much I need this. And I mean for a number of reasons. But mainly because I need my plan to work, and it will not work without a job. Do I want to execute my plan right under his scrutinizing nose? No, but there is a great deal of benefit here. Making him see me in a different, more intellectual light and excelling in an area that he holds great respect for gives me an upper hand in my ridiculous yet devious plan. I'm sure he doesn't know that, but what does it matter? We're both after something. My something is survival. His something is…money? Revenge? I'm not sure yet, but I'll find out.

Moving forward.

"Melissa, I appreciate your effort, but I may need a little more than that."

I squint my eyes just slightly so as not to be too overt about my suspicion, but enough to express without words that I am not fearful of the direction that he is taking this conversation in. "Angelo, why am I interviewing with you?"

He tilts his head. "All interviews typically serve one purpose, Melissa. You know that. So you'll need to elaborate on your question."

"Did everyone else come in here in this office and sit at this desk to answer your questions?" I'm not sure how much more elaborate he wants me to be.

"No."

"So there's a reason then that I'm here. With you?"

"Yes."

"What exactly is that reason?"

"Well, your resume—"

"Bullshit." Yeah, not the best choice of word to use in the midst of an interview, but what's done is done. I lean forward. "My resume says nothing about science. I took your class. You've seen my grades as you've mentioned, yet here I am. Here we are. Why am I here if you knew that you were just going to ask me questions that amplify the truth that we were both already aware of?"

He now leans forward. "Because you have potential."

I roll my eyes and look away, unsatisfied with his lackluster response.

"Look at me."

I turn his way, unsure of why all my defiance just abandoned my body with his sudden shift in tone. I'm stronger than this, yet his eyes are piercing my soul. Something is wrong with me. There has to be something wrong with me because I am unbelievably turned on right now.

I lick my lips.

"I need to know that you're aware of your potential. I cannot bring you in here with an ounce of doubt leaking from your pores, emanating off your aura or betraying you with your own eyes. This is forensics. We work directly with the FBI. You need to be completely aware of your capabilities."

Have I mentioned how piercing his eyes are?

We're both breathing slightly heavier than we were when this interview began.

Or maybe it's just me.

"Is this something you think you can do? I need to know now, Melissa."

Chapter Seven

Angelo

I cannot very well tell her that she is walking into her grave. That I brought her here to tell her she got the job only to get her close enough to me to trust me. With her trust, I wouldn't have to take her life, because she'd give it to me. I could tell her that I don't want her money, but I want to be the cause of the loss of her peace of mind. I want her mental stability in the palm of my hands, because her noble father ripped both right out from underneath me. Her family made my family and I eat shit, figuratively speaking.

I also cannot just give her the job either, because despite her age, she is, like I've said, inquisitive and witty, as you know. So I posted a need for this position, getting a flock of empty-minded students for my staff to ask generic interview questions, only to turn down each and every one of them.

CONFIDENT SENSUALITY

So I tell her she has potential because at the end of the day, after I take back what her father took, my reputation is still on the line. I still need to justify bringing her on board instead of the other overqualified students. I need her to take this seriously so that I can carry out my plan effectively.

"All I can tell you, Angelo, is that if I'm given an opportunity, I'll put forth my best efforts. My pride is far too profound to drop the ball. However, I am still learning. This internship would be great, but as much as this field fascinates me, I genuinely don't have applicable knowledge about forensics."

"That's why I will be your mentor."

"I'm sorry?"

"You heard me."

"Say it again."

I look at her, threatening her defiance with my ego.

In short, we're both stubborn. Her stubbornness, however, holds more emotion. That makes her a little more transparent than she'd like to be.

So I can see her facade falter a bit when I look at her like I'd like to devour her. Make that stubborn shield of hers crumble like a puddle at her feet.

We're interrupted by a knock.

"Come in," I call without taking my eyes off her.

One of my current interns, Sampson, who is in his last year of undergrad, sticks his head into my office to tell me I have a call on line two.

Sampson is an African American with a low fade haircut and a football player's frame. He has a rather warm and kind demeanor and nice teeth, so the ladies at this office thoroughly enjoy speaking with him.

"Thanks, Sam."

"Not a problem." He looks at Melissa, smiles, waves, and then proceeds to introduce himself.

"Sampson. That's an awesome name," she tells him. "My name's Melissa."

"Thank you, Melissa. It's a pleasure to meet you."

"You as well, Sampson." She says his name slowly, on purpose, of course.

"Are the two of you finished?"

Sampson, at least, has the decency to look apologetic. "Sorry, sir. You guys have a great day." He closes the door.

"He seems nice." She's smirking at me. Everything is a fucking game for her.

"Monday morning, 6:00 a.m. sharp. Business attire. Purchase a lab jacket because we will not be providing you one."

CONFIDENT SENSUALITY

She sits up straighter, simultaneously ridding her face of that smirk. "What?"

"You heard me," I state, gathering my paperwork. I begin walking around my desk to see her out so I can take my call on line two in private.

But Melissa has plans of her own; she corners me. Her left hand rises to land on my wayward curls. She runs her fingers through them, breathing my air. Her right hand lands on my chest. Then, her relentless smirk returns to her freckled face.

Freckles.

She has freckles.

"Say it again, Angelo."

I control my breathing, because...because this is inappropriate. "Melissa," I start.

She steps closer. "So I got the job?" she whispers, smiling. This smile holds warmth.

I clear my throat. "Yes."

"Just say it." Her lips are a hair away from mine. Her warm breath heats my lips, making my dick a fucking traitor.

I clear my throat again. "You got the job, Melissa."

Her right hand falls from my chest, allowing me to reclaim some of my breath. Her left hand follows, leaving me feeling oddly cold.

"Thank you," she says. She starts backing away, keeping her eyes on me and forcing a slew of thoughts to flood my brain. Each of said thoughts are warnings, and suddenly I can't hear anything outside of the alarms sounding in my head. Thinking effectively is no longer an option.

You don't get to walk away from me, Melissa.

Before I have a chance to deny myself, my arms are reaching for her. I feel like I'm moving in slow motion, yet she ends up flushed against my chest in seconds. My fingers lace through her hair at the base of her skull. I tilt her head up toward me, brushing my lips against hers. "Don't tease me, Melissa."

Then her lips become mine. Her soft, succulent, plump lips become mine. I'm kissing and sucking and biting until she opens up, and our tongues begin to dance. I pick her up and put her on my desk, dragging her hips toward my pulsing core so she can feel what she does to me when she plays these fucking games.

She sucks on my bottom lip, moaning into my mouth every time I massage her core. I'm losing my mind. We need to stop. We should stop. She pushes her breasts into my chest, so I take my cue, trailing my hand up her shirt.

CONFIDENT SENSUALITY

Knock, knock. "Fuck." I pull away from her, breathing as if she has removed every ounce of breath from my body.

I look at her with her "fuck me" eyes and her swollen lips.

She stands abruptly, adjusting herself, and finally says, "I'll see you Monday morning at six."

Knock, knock. Melissa makes her way to the door, opening it to where Sampson stands. "Hello again," he says.

Melissa, in a cheerful voice, responds with "Hi there!"

He watches her walk away, so I clear my throat, bringing him back to my less-than-cheerful face. "You knocked," I remind him.

"Oh. Uh, yeah. Line two hung up and called back. She's on hold for you again."

"Thank you."

"No pro—"

I close my office door, walking over to my phone to answer the terror that awaits on the other side of line two.

"This is Angelo."

"Where the fuck is my child?" Ah, there she is. That fiery French accent brings back so many memories.

"Well, hello there."

"Answer my question."

"I don't fall slave to anyone's commands, but if you must know, she's very pleased to be my new employee."

"Listen to me." Her voice drops an octave or two. "If there is a single scratch on my baby, your life will come to a slow, painful end."

"Is that so?"

"You know what I can do. Do not test me."

"Test you? Is that what you think I'm doing?" I release a short laugh. "I would never do such a heinous thing. This is not a test, Lisa. Everything I do serves a rather distinct purpose. So not to worry, my dear sweet Lisa. I am most certainly not testing you."

My phone meets its receiver.

Chapter Eight

Melissa

I'm walking to my jeep, replaying every second of my interview with Angelo, right up to the point where he devoured my lips. If Sampson didn't knock, would I have just let him have his way with me?

He kissed me like he was starving and I was his first meal. Is this how this whole operation should start? I didn't give him a chance to change his mind about offering me the job. I bolted out of his office without another interaction lest he came to his senses, acknowledging the madness that just took place. I also already called my mother and told her I got the job prior to the actual interview. Can you blame me? Her precious niece, Ramona, held so many accomplishments under her belt, and every time we spoke, somehow a comparison of the two of us found its way into the conversation. I just wanted something to childishly rub in Ramona's face in addition to having the opportunity to get my mother out of my ass about what direction my life was headed in.

Her response was lackluster. I wasn't surprised.

She'd asked, "Forensics? You want to get into that?"

I rolled my eyes. "What's wrong with forensic science? This internship is a great opportunity, Mother."

"Yes, I'm sure it is, but with you having just barely passed your most recent science course, I'm not sure how you're going to make it through this internship."

"Being in the field is completely different from being in the classroom. You know this."

"Well, yes, but—"

"I'm happy that I've been able to at least get my career started prior to my graduation. Was Ramona able to do that?" That was a juvenile question to ask, but her lack of support stung. "She has all these awards, but where are her interviews, Mother?"

"That's not the point."

"We'll discuss the point later."

I hung up.

My mother and I have always had an interesting relationship to say the least, but lately, there has been more of a strain. Everything I say seems to be the wrong thing to say. I shrug to myself, starting up my car, getting Lacey on my Bluetooth because someone is going to be happy for me, dammit.

"Yo!"

"Have you made it back home yet?"

"Nope, and I'm in no rush. I might get crazy and go below the speed limit."

"Wow. Not so stoked to see the family?"

"Am I ever?"

"True."

"So what's the deal? You get the dick or nah?"

She wastes no time. I shake my head as if she can see me. "Not quite."

"Okay, bitch. What does that mean? Was he small?"

"No, Lace—"

"Was he trash?"

"Listen, he—"

"He was trash, wasn't he?"

"Lacey, I—"

"All that smolder put to waste. It's a damn shame."

"Lacey! He kissed me!"

"So…no dick?"

"No, bitch."

"Elaborate."

I fill her in.

"Wait, so he kissed you?"

I smile as if she can see me. "Yeah."

"You sneaky bitch. Well done."

"So I start Monday."

"Fuck yeah, you do!"

I laugh. "I'm a little nervous."

"Don't be. Angelo knows you don't know shit about forensics."

"That's not what I meant."

"Oh."

"I don't really know where to go from here… romance-wise. The kiss was great, but do you think it happened too soon? I don't want him misplacing my intentions. Then he won't take me seriously, and the whole operation will be blown to—"

"Whoa, whoa, whoa. I think maybe you need to trust yourself a little more."

She's right.

"However, mind your emotions."

"Mind my emotions." I repeat her words, insinuating that an explanation is desired.

"Don't get too caught up in the plan. You'll lose control of everything else. Stay calm. Stay focused."

CONFIDENT SENSUALITY

She leaves me with those words of wisdom and kicks me off the phone since she blames me for missing two of her exits.

In pulling up to my destination, I realized that I forgot to tell her that I ran into Candace.

My phone buzzes, and with my assumption that it's Lacey, I answered.

"Melissa."

It is not Lacey. It's my loving cousin. "Ramona."

"Mom's upset, and I'm sure it has something to do with you."

"Well, for starters, she's not your mother. She's your aunt."

"Right, because only biological kids can upset their parents the way you upset your mom. She's never been this upset over anything I've done. So I'm sure you're happy to know that you've upset your mother. Well done."

She hangs up.

This is fucking perfect.

My mother was behind this. She just has to be in control. My mother never gets upset about anything. Nothing. Ramona, however, will do anything she asks because Ramona prides herself in being up my mother's ass. I'm not really certain who my mother thinks I am, but she may have forgotten that I'm in the midst of becoming someone separate from her little girl. So that shit does not work on me anymore. She may have hoped that I'd call her, console her, and nurse her ego back to life, but I'm so far removed from the manipulation that this family breeds.

Chapter Nine

Lisa

Angelo seems to be under the impression that he can just have my child.

My precious Melissa.

He also seems to have forgotten who I am. I don't get angry very often, as I need to have a precise grip on what takes place around me. Hence the reason I raised an incredible woman. Make no mistake, she is not beneath the challenge he thinks he's posed. I've prepared her for this. She knows four languages: French, Italian, Spanish, and English. Lorenzo knows each one of said languages fluently; she would always know what he's planning despite his potential intent to hide it via communicating with his foreign colleagues. This will keep her ahead of the game.

I even made her help me with framing her father. She had no idea that I killed him. Absolutely none. But that was the best way to expose her to the life she was born into. She was setting up a scene to make it look like a mother was only protecting herself and her children. These skills don't just disappear. I taught her how to be manipulative. However, one can only be manipulative if they're confident in their own character, so I always remind her of who she is and push her to accomplish more.

Simplicity is not enough.

Mediocrity is not enough.

I just wish she had more men in her life. That would have been her time to shine; my child is stunning. She would have mastered the art of manipulation if she'd just stepped out her box and lured some of these empty-headed college boys into her life for a bit.

Nevertheless, she had the most expensive tutors so I could send her to Brown's University. I wanted my child to have a haughty air about her for attending such a prestigious university and then earn it when she got the education. I always told her, "If you present yourself a certain way, you attract certain people." And she did. She attracted my friend, Sebastien Angelo. Something about her caught his eye, and then recognition set in. Sebastien is right where I want him: in the palm of my daughter's hands.

I know who I am, and although I'm not proud of it, I'm not apologetic either. I don't want her to know who I am just yet. And I know Sebastien won't tell her because Angelo is a man of his word. A man that sticks to his plan. Telling her would throw a wrench in it. That simple fact gives me time and puts her ahead of the game.

She just needs to put all that I've taught her to use. That will inevitably have him sitting nice and pretty on the bull's-eye.

I'll just need to take my shot.

"What did she say?" I now ask my niece, Ramona.

"Not much. She doesn't care, Mom."

"I don't believe that. Of course, she cares. I'm her mother. We're family."

Ramona rolls her eyes. "She's not going to see things the way you do. Or the way you want her to. The way I do."

"She may not see things now, but she will, honey."

She looks at me, aghast.

"Trust me."

"I do trust you. But..." She shrugs, as if to say 'tis a lost cause but continues anyway. "I think she's going to betray you."

"Why?" I'm trying not to lose my patience. I do, however, need to draw the line at some point.

"This Angelo guy? She's going to fall in love with him. And then everything that you've invested in will be pointless."

"How dare you? This discussion is over." My plan is thorough. Not a *t* uncrossed.

She gets up from our plush living room couch. "You can believe what you want, but I'm more invested in this operation that she ever will be, and you know that."

"Enough!"

Ramona

She's still yelling, but I've made myself scarce. She'll see soon enough that I'm the only one supporting her.

Melissa is not interested in this family. She's always been more independent, and by independent, I mean removed, distant, uninterested. I have always been more invested in the welfare of this family. Mom thinks Melissa will have a come-to moment where she realizes that this family is all she needs.

She won't.

I'll be there when the moment of betrayal is all Lisa has to look at. She'll then turn to me, and I'll be everything she needs.

She will finally see Melissa for who she is.

That moment, however, is not the one I'm looking forward.

Melissa still has no idea what she's been born into, what future awaits her, or how her father passed.

That moment of truth is coming. She thinks she's been running away from it, but she's walking right into the inevitable truth. Her heart will be broken. Her world will be shattered. She will finally feel betrayed.

She will feel what I've felt, what I feel now, watching Mom choose her every time over me.

Chapter Ten

Melissa

Day one on the job.

I had my bowl of Wheaties and purchased a lab coat that was far too expensive, but it looks better than Stacy's, so there's a small victory already.

I walk right up to Angelo's office door with high hopes and low expectations.

Who am I kidding?

My nerves are betraying me. I can feel moisture in my armpits, my tights are too tight, and my shoes, despite its cuteness, will not uphold its comfortability throughout the day. Honestly, the only thing that was on my mind this morning while I was getting dressed was the kiss.

Lacey's words replay in my head: "Stay calm. Stay focused."

Then he opens the door.

CONFIDENT SENSUALITY

He smells like a fresh shower; his hair definitely looks like he just stepped out of the shower. I still want to put my fingers in—

"Are you through ogling?"

"What? I was not ogling."

He steps aside to let me in, already moving past my denial.

I was definitely ogling.

I walk ahead of him, his words lingering behind me. "There are a few orientation things I'd like to go over and paperwork you need to sign, and then we can discuss what your responsibilities are going to be here."

Okay, so we're not going to address the kiss. I don't know if this is relief or disappointment. Either way, I'm internally deflating.

I fill out all the tax paperwork and some legal documents, basically reinforcing my need to respect the privacy of each case by refraining from discussing any aspects with anyone who isn't already working on the case.

The office door creeks, and the familiar pleasant voice of Sampson gives me a sense of ease. "Mr. Angelo, you have a—"

Angelo's hand meets the desk with brute force. "Do *not* enter my office without my permission."

Sampson, however, does not flinch. Instead, what he does is offer a curt nod and state, "My apologies, sir. You have another call. Sounds like the same client from last week." And with that, he makes his departure.

I turn back to Angelo. "You're slightly more cranky than usual."

He says nothing.

"Oh, I know what it is," I continue coaxing.

Silence.

"You're on your monthly menstrual cycle, aren't you?" I'm poking the bear. And I'm actually looking forward to his unleashing, so to speak. Anything would be better than his indifference for Christ's sake.

"Melissa, please be sure to attend to your paperwork while I handle my responsibilities."

In other words, mind your damn business.

"Is this the kind of demeanor I'll have to deal with for the duration of this internship, or do I have the option to be placed with someone else? Someone slightly more chipper?" I grab a mint from his little fancy candy jar on his desk while maintaining my line of vision with the top of his head, since he's not paying me or my questions any attention.

I'm prepared to continue asking questions though.

He continues to refuse to acknowledge my inquiries, so I proceed with another question. "I was also wondering—"

"Melissa." He finally meets my eyes.

I smile sweetly at him. "Yes, honey."

"Let's first address how I will be addressed. I am still Professor Angelo."

"Interesting."

"Moving forward—"

"I'd like to address the kiss."

"What kiss?"

I know what he's trying to do, but I'm surprised that feigning ignorance is the way he chooses to do it. However, if he wants to play, I'll play too. "If you don't remember, I'll be happy to jog your memory."

He stares at me.

Fine. "The one thing I remember the most is how your tongue felt against mine."

He clears his throat.

I raise an eyebrow. "Should I continue?"

Nothing.

I shrug. "You tasted like mint and chocolate." I stand up, maintaining eye contact while also continuing my verbal seduction. "But as enticing as your tongue was, your hands were my favorite part.

Actually, more specifically, your fingers, especially when they were tugging on my nip—"

"Stop."

I stare at him, taunting. "Stop what? What's done is done. All I'm doing is giving you a play by play since you've somehow contracted a sudden case of amnesia."

"Melissa, if you cannot be professional—"

"Then what? You're going to fire me? Allow me to remind you, Angelo, *you* kissed *me*."

He stands.

"You have always prided yourself in being a man of your word. What kind of man would you be if you fired me because of a decision you made?"

He walks around his desk and over to me. "I understand."

Say what? My head jerks back, and I kick myself mentally, because I have grown to despise showing emotion around this man.

"It would be rather juvenile of me to terminate your employment here on a decision that I made. Except when I kissed you"—he grabs my chin, tilting my head up toward his mouth—"you seemed to have been kissing me back. In fact, your deep-throated moans were a pretty strong indication that you were enjoying it, were you not?"

CONFIDENT SENSUALITY

Fuck.

How did we arrive here?

I was teasing him.

Yet here we stand with him having the upper hand and my chin in his hand.

Does he want me to kiss him? Would that be too much? Would I seem too desperate if I do kiss him? Is he just setting me up?

The truth of the matter is, I want to kiss him. I would love to put my fingers in his hair again and have his lips wrapped around my nipples again. However, the only way I see myself getting what I want and coming out on top is if I find a way to make him beg for it. That would have to mean depriving myself of my desires right now. I step back. His hand drops from my chin. "You're right. I enjoyed every second of it." My eye contact is steady. For now.

"So you agree?" I don't know if that was shock that I heard in his voice, but I think I've gained some sort of upper hand in this equation.

He continues, "It wasn't an individual decision, correct? It was also driven by your desire."

I shrug. "Sure. I'll do my best to stay professional."

He stares at me for a beat too long, nods, and says, "All right. Let's get to work."

We continue to go over policies and procedures, expectations, boundaries, and all the other jazz that falls within that category.

The day seems to drag on with orientation and introductions. I have yet, however, to gain clarification on what my responsibilities are. So I ask, "What do you want from me?"

"Excuse me?"

I nearly roll my eyes. "What will my daily tasks be? What is the actual job description? I mean, I am still a student, but this is also still my job. And I still don't know what I'm supposed to be doing." I know he is aware of that, but I don't understand the origin of his incredulousness.

"I will get to that, Melissa. One step at a time. Being hired is a process." He's very good at sounding intolerant.

"You're not a man of many words. I mean you're articulate, but you don't speak much. There is no language for brooding, Angelo."

He stares at me, proving my point. "So we got the politics down," I continue, "but the more simple questions still remain without answers."

He continues to stare at me. This time, I do roll my eyes.

Chapter Eleven

Angelo

Today has been interesting, to say the least. Melissa has been studying me since the beginning of our day. And by me, I mean my every move, everything I have and have not said, my temperament, and the color of my fucking eyes.

I was explaining the term *adnexa* to her in reference to how it coincides with forensics science. During my explanation, I'd alternate looking at her and the list of forensic-related terms, until she stopped me simply to say "The shade of your eyes fluctuates based on your emotions."

What the fuck? "Excuse me."

"You're clearly very passionate about forensic science." She became very serious, less… What's the correct word I'm looking for? Less mischievous.

"Okay."

"So your eyes," she continued, reaching up to trail her finger over my right eyebrow, "are a deeper shade of green. It's almost as if the passion is swallowing the hue, and I, as a result, have to look very closely to catch the hint of green that is still trying to shine through." Her voice was just above a whisper.

Her hand created a trail from my brow to my jaw, ending at the corners of my lips. My dick betrayed me, standing on attention.

She then withdrew her hand, sat back, and shrugged. Her concluding statement was "I just thought that was cool."

Great.

"Thank you for sharing, Melissa." I had deadpanned.

She smiled. "Of course."

My dick twitched. My face remained the same, yet somehow, I feel that that sweet smile of hers was an indication or a message, so to speak, from her to me that she was in fact aware of what had just transpired. And she was very pleased with herself.

Touché.

*****

My office phone rings now, ripping through the room. I'd say it was my "saved by the bell" moment, but judging by the line that is lighting up, I would say I'm simply jumping from the pot into the fire.

Her mother has been trying, to no avail, to get in touch with me since our last exchange of loving words. We have nothing to discuss. She is fully aware that her daughter belongs to me now.

"This is Angelo."

"Well, hello there, sweetheart."

"I'll be more than happy to discuss business with you at a later time. I am currently with a student. If none of your matters are urgent, we will have to reschedule this call."

"Oops. Now wait a minute, honey. We don't have very much to discuss. Scene one act one is done. Let's just skip right to the climax, shall we? My daughter isn't in danger. You are."

I nearly laugh. She does this. She's very overt in her manipulation. She's okay with telling you her plan, only after she's through with that phase.

Everything is planned, and every tactic has its moment to be utilized. Once that part of the plan has come and gone, the tactic becomes useless. On to the next.

"That's very interesting news," I respond. "I'm glad you've called to share this with me. However, I would like to get back to my student."

"I know she's there." Her voice is calm, a stark contrast to the frantic woman I spoke with just a few days ago. "You should have gone into acting. Your chances of making it there far exceed your chances of surviving this internship with my perfect child. You've no idea what you've started, Sebastien."

I laugh. "Thank you for that bout of humor. I look forward to speaking with you later."

The call is terminated.

"That was a weird business call."

Her sixth sense may be the death of me. Nonetheless, I'll just have to be more mindful of my actions and my body language.

"Were you faking the funk with that one?" She deposits a short laugh into the room.

"Yeah, she isn't particularly my favorite colleague. But maturity can sometimes call for a bit of facetious behavior, ironically."

She shrugs. "I suppose." She looks down at her nails. "You seem to be shifting moods quite a bit today."

I tilt my head, unsure of how to respond. I have lost my head one too many times today. I blame myself. I shouldn't have kissed her so soon. I need to stay focused, and unfortunately, I've allowed said recent events to dictate my actions.

CONFIDENT SENSUALITY

I felt that I had things under control for the vast majority of the day, but it feels like things are slipping through the grip that isn't as tight as I would have hoped.

"I just have several things taking place at one time, all of which have deadlines very close in range."

She shakes her head, almost as if to say "Tsk, that's not enough."

"I don't know, Angelo," she starts. "The past fifteen weeks held absolutely no outbursts like the ones you had today."

I shouldn't be surprised; she has always been this outspoken, never afraid to hit the nail on the head. But today, right now, she seems to be aiming to hit something else. "I'm in a different setting with different stressors."

"True."

She's not finished.

"But…"

I knew it.

"I guess my question is, am I one of your deadlines? One of your added stressors?"

What she'd like to know is whether or not she's distracting me. She wants the satisfaction of knowing that she has an effect on me. I feel that she already knows the obvious aspect of it. I'm a man, and she's an attractive woman, so there will be sexual tension. However, we are two mature adults who can work through this with self-control, excluding our initial mishap.

Until it's time for me to use it to my advantage, of course.

"We're attracted to one another, but we are adults, Melissa."

"Bullshit."

I should have known better. "I am still your boss. I need you to not only mind your tone but your language as well. Professionalism is—"

"Listen, Angelo. You can pretend all you'd like and give me speeches on professionalism until the cows come home…"

A short laugh escapes my lips.

"But you already know the truth," she continues.

"Enlighten me."

Knock, knock.

Fucking Sampson. "Come in."

"Professor Angelo." Interestingly enough, it's Stacy.

She steps into my office, exposing more of her professional attire, no doubt for Melissa to see. "I have some documents for you to sign. We just need approval on a few things."

"Well, hello there, Stacey." Melissa is utilizing her best teasing tone, but I simply shake my head with no intent to interject.

Stacy utters her name with a profound amount of bitterness. "Melissa."

"Thank you, Stacy. I'll have them ready by tomorrow," I cut in.

She turns to leave with a curt nod.

"Thanks, Stacy," Melissa calls after her.

My office door slams shut, Melissa collapses in laughter. "Ugh. I cannot wait to tell Lacey this."

I stare at her disapprovingly. "Why is it so difficult for you to be professional?"

She doesn't bat an eyelash or falter for one second with her response. "Professional," she repeats the word slowly, almost as if to get a better taste of it. "You throw that word around an awful lot. But I get it. I'll try to have more interactions like the one you had today with Sampson, because *that* was professionalism at its finest."

What a blow to the fucking chest. "I need my authority to be respected."

"Right, and that was the way to do it professionally. An open act of jealousy is exactly the kind of professionalism I hope to achieve someday."

"An open act of jealousy." It's my turn to see how the words taste on my tongue. "So you've presumed that I'm jealous."

"Yes."

I stand up, rolling up my sleeves to the forearms. I unbutton my collar and push the hair that was once taking residence on my forehead out of the way. "That is quite an interesting take on the situation."

"Call it what you want. You know my points are valid." Her breathing pattern has changed. It's always cute when she thinks she can outplay this game with me. I am the master of this game.

I shrug, sliding my hands in my pocket to keep from reaching for her. She licks her full, plush lips when she's nervous, and she's done it at least ten times within the past two minutes.

"Am I making you nervous?"

"No." She stands abruptly, bending down to pick up her belongings. "What time do I need to be here tomorrow? Are we going to be doing the same thing?"

I walk over to her while she places her things in her bag and place my hands on her hips. She startles and drops her things. But she doesn't move away, so my grip become slightly tighter, and I lean into her neck and inhale her infectious scent. I trail my tongue from the base of her slender neck to her pulse and plant a soft kiss there. "Why do you think I'm jealous?"

Her breathing is heavier. "Um." Her voice is unsteady. "Because…" And she can't find her words. Just the way I like it.

She's in the palm of my hands, right where she should be. "Because you are," she continues. I can tell she wanted to say that with more gusto. Poor thing.

I trail my lips to her shoulder and plant soft kisses. She may be aggressive and outspoken, but she's so very soft on the inside. That's what will allow me to come out on top of this forsaken game.

"Are you sure?" My hand slides to cup her left breast, and a small moan escapes those perfect fucking lips; we're so close to her undoing. Sampson better not come bestow a single knock on my office door. I need this so things can finally take off in the direction that I'd like them to. I need her to feel like she needs me.

She takes my hand suddenly and snakes it under her shirt, covering her breast with it. I take over from there, undoing her bra and pinching those taut nipples between my fingers. Her head falls back against my chest, and I take my free hand to grab her neck and tilt her head just enough for me to taste her neck just a little more before I take what is mine.

Her moans start making my pants tighter. I remove her blouse forcefully, dislodging some buttons. She inhales sharply, driving me completely insane. Her breathy moans and her intoxicating scent are making it difficult to stay in control. She takes her pencil skirt off and pushes me back onto my desk, taking my clothes off with purpose, and I have no intention of stopping her.

She's now standing before me completely naked. Striking.

My pants are still on, but it's quite evident that I'd prefer them to be off.

"Take them off," she demands.

I stand slowly, maintaining eye contact, and remove my pants. My erection springs free, and she places a hand on my chest, pushing me back down onto my desk. And then she does it. She fucking straddles me and seats herself completely onto me, gliding down every inch. I close my eyes, and my head falls back when she grips my hair at the base of my skull, finally beginning to ride me.

This is ecstasy.

I feel her warm breath on my lips, so I anticipate a kiss, but instead she whispers, "You're a jealous man, Angelo."

Nothing but moans escape my throat.

"Say it," she whispers.

I'm lost in a frenzy of sensation.

She rides me just a little faster. "Please," she whimpers.

Fuck me. "I'm jealous. I don't want him near you." I grab her hips, controlling her movements. "I don't want him thinking about touching you."

"Why? Because you want to be the only one touching me?"

I stand up and flip us around, putting her on the desk, diving into her. Every thrust holds an intent to go deeper. Her moans are gaining volume, so I cover her mouth and lean in, demanding that she look at me. I slow my thrusts, making her whimper her disapproval.

"It doesn't matter if I'm jealous," I whisper. "I'm still your boss, and you won't be communicating with him from this point."

Part of me wants him to hear me driving into her, making her moan, making her mine. I want it made clear to her and to her counterparts who she belongs to.

Her leg starts to shake, and her back is arching. "Please," she whimpers again. I thrust harder with every plea until she crumbles beneath me, taking me with her completely over the edge.

I collapse on top of her limp body, with our breaths colliding. "Well damn." She laughs, trailing her fingers up and down my spine.

I stand abruptly, making her startle. Her eyes come into focus on my naked form. "Clean yourself up." I hand her her clothing. "I expect you here tomorrow at 7:00 a.m. sharp."

She takes it from me, avoiding eye contact.

I pull on my clothes haphazardly and make myself scarce so she can get dressed.

As I'm finishing up donning my attire, I turn around, and she's struggling with her bra.

She's crying.

Fuck me.

What? I can't go over there and console her. She has to work through this herself.

She looks up at me, and all I can see is her strength.

I see her square her shoulders.

She maintains her eye contact with me, threatening to unleash something inside of me that I am certain was buried a long time ago.

I hope that within her search for light in my soul, she recognizes the unrelenting darkness that overwhelms each spec of light that tries and fails to break free. She'll be disappointed because I am and will always be a man of my word. I made a promise that stemmed directly from my darkness, and I will carry it out. I am not who she is searching for.

She finishes up getting dressed and sees herself out of my office, brushing past a now smug Stacy.

"How can I help you?" I ask as she now steps into my office.

Her smug appearance disappears when she hears the evident annoyance in my tone.

"I was just checking to see if you needed anything."

Oh, for fuck's sake. "No."

She rolls her eyes and storms out, slamming my office door.

Chapter Twelve

Melissa

"You've gotta be fucking kidding me." Lacey, as you can tell, is very unhappy with the recent span of events that I've had to endure.

She's still visiting family.

I asked her if it was a good time to talk, and she'd said, "I don't really give a shit whether or not it's a good time to talk. Now talk."

So now we're talking.

"So wait," she continues, "you guys sexed. Was it good?"

I exhaled dramatically. "Lacey, that is not the point."

"It may not be the point, but it is most certainly one of them."

I mumble a "yes."

"I'm sorry. One more time for my Asian ears."

"Yes, bitch. It was spectacular."

"Aw shit."

"I know."

"No. I don't think you do. See, all you've ever had was Roderick's trash dick. Your anger and your hurt are both currently preventing you from realizing the long-term damage. Good dick is the devil."

"How would you know? You're gay. You haven't been within five feet of dick. Much less good dick."

"Any good sexual encounter will have a grown woman with class acting rather strange."

"But—"

"But it goes both ways. If you enjoyed it, chances are high that he did as well. So here's the plan. Since you left there in tears, you have to walk back in there void of emotion."

"Void?"

"Void," she repeats. "As in the absence of."

"Yes, I know what it means. I'm saying I'm clearly incapable of hiding my emotions."

"Temporarily."

I squint my eyes in question as if she can see me. "I'm lost."

"You didn't fall in love with him, so you'll recover quickly. But if you walk in there after this little Christmas break we have and you don't still look broken up about it, believe it or not, it'll fuck with his manhood. And he won't recover quickly."

The little Christmas break for me is literally the day before Christmas and Christmas Day since I'm a working woman now.

"So," I start, "that's when the war is declared, when I begin to act emotionally removed?"

"Boom, baby." She's silent for a minute, which was a strong indication that she was about to delve slightly deeper into my sudden outburst of tears after having been so confident in my game-playing ability. Or it was an indication that she was about to dish out a great deal of "I told you so."

We'll see.

"How'd you lose your shit so quick?" she questions. *I knew it.* "I mean he's an ass, and what he did was an asshole thing to do, yes. But we went into this knowing it was a game. What happened? For real."

"Honestly, it was just such a major blow to my ego. I was mad at him and a little hurt but even more upset with myself because I slipped up. And then I spiraled down that road of doubt. Like why did I get myself into this in the first place? He's clearly better at this ridiculous game than I am. I felt like I was setting myself up."

"For what?"

CONFIDENT SENSUALITY

"You're right," I continue my point, almost dismissing her question. "I am not in love, so I will recover. But I'm nervous that this whole thing will blow up in my face. That he'll come out on top, and I come up missing."

"Nah."

"That's it?"

"From what you told me, you're not the only one on a slippery slope of feelings."

"No. I disagree. I think this entire thing is a sick game for him."

"It definitely is, but—"

"No. I mean, I believe he's been playing before I even decided to join." Realization is setting in. "And him telling me about my father was an open invitation. It was a setup, and I fell for it. As a matter of fact, I've likely been a prop in his game for a while. He—"

"I got it, Mel."

"Right. I'm just saying he will always have the upper hand."

"I get what you're saying, I do, but I doubt he expected you to choose to fight back the way you're fighting. I do not believe he was able to foresee you planning to make him fall for you. This is just a little hiccup. You've learned, and you're in too deep to back out now. So get out of your head and get in the game."

"Fine."

I need a new approach. At this point, I don't think making him fall for me should be the game plan. Perhaps making him beg for me is the better alternative.

"When are you coming back?" I ask, suddenly eager to discuss something else.

"Literally the day after Christmas."

"You're not staying until the New Year?"

"Absolutely not."

I ask her about being home; she hates it just as much as she did the last time I asked.

I shrug. "Well, we need to go shopping. I need more new work clothes."

"What? Didn't you just get new clothes?"

"Yeah. But my motive has changed, and I'd like my wardrobe to reflect that."

She laughs. "Sure."

*****

Christmas comes and goes.

CONFIDENT SENSUALITY

I called home to wish my mother and Ramona a Merry Christmas. I'm usually really big on that kind of stuff. I love Christmas shopping, gift wrapping, the whole shebang. But I've been a little preoccupied with trying to save lives and win manipulative mind games or whatever. You know, the usual.

Anyways, the conversation, as I'm sure you can already imagine, didn't go very well.

"Melissa." Ramona answered the phone.

"Merry Christmas." The words flew out of my mouth. Straight to the chase. No conversation necessary. "Where's my mom?"

"She doesn't want to speak with you."

I roll my eyes. "Just give her the phone."

"Melissa, darling. How are you?" Doesn't sound like she doesn't want to speak with me.

"Hey, Ma. Just calling to wish you a Merry Christmas."

"Well, Merry Christmas. It'd be nice if you were here to celebrate with us."

"I know, but you know I just got this job, and I may actually be starting at a coffee shop soon."

"Two jobs. Wait a minute, why do you need them both? What's the purpose of working at the coffee shop?"

"I don't really like having to depend on you for money." Whoa. No idea where those words came from.

"Melissa, I'm your mother. It's okay to depend on me."

"Okay, but for how long?"

She was silent for a minute. "Well…"

"I'm just trying not to set myself up. Knowing that you're there sort of made me devalue hard work." My exact thoughts were *Who the fuck am I?*

"Really? Well, I was under the impression that I taught you the value of hard work."

"How?"

Silence.

"Mom, you've taught me—us—a lot. But some things can't be taught. Some things I may just have to walk right into to learn."

"Like what? What things?"

I pulled the phone away from my ear and stared at it for a bit, hoping maybe it can offer an explanation for what was transpiring. "Mom, all I'm saying is, I value the process. It was nice buying my own clothes. It was just nice knowing that the money I was spending was coming from my wallet, and I earned the opportunity to be able to spend it." That was well said, if I do say so myself.

CONFIDENT SENSUALITY

"Whatever you're hiding, Melissa, I'll find out."

I rolled my eyes. "Seriously? Okay, Mother. Well, when you figure it out, let me know." I hung up.

Now I'm sitting in the living room with Lacey, who's ecstatic to be back, and Candace, who's also glad Lacey is back, going through my new selection of clothing.

"Damn, your mom is really going through it." Lacey responds to my recap of the conversation with my mother.

"Maybe she just misses you," Candace adds.

I shake my head. "My mom's always been a little strange, for lack of a better word, but lately she's been…paranoid."

"Did you ask her for any money or make any small references to the shit show you're in with Angelo?"

"Nah. At least I don't think so."

Lacey shrugs. "Welp, we've got bigger fish to fry, bitch. We need a plan for Sir Mafia Lord Angelo."

Candace rolls her eyes.

I dump the contents of my recent shopping spree on the couch. I have a pantsuit that fits snug around the waist and ass region and is loose toward the bottom. I don't think I'm going to wear the blazer that comes with it because I want my figure to show, and the blazer may mask it a bit.

"Oh, this is super cute," Candace declares, pulling out my leather skirt. It's a high-waist, knee length, form-fitting—

"Bitch, that looks expensive. Your first check must have been spectacular."

Lacey works at a doctor's office part-time and saves her pennies as she refuses to ask her family for anything. So I know she's going to mention my recklessness as far as finances are concerned.

"I know, I know. After this, I'll start saving, but these outfits are fueling my gusto. Or my lack thereof."

She pulls out more expensive pieces, gawking and commenting on my boldness both in finance and attitude.

"So what's the plan?" Candace asks.

"She's going to go in there tomorrow," Lacey begins, "with the most professional approach. No mentions of the"—she forms air quotes with her fingers—"acts of sex."

Candace rolls her eyes. "So you're going to let him off the hook?"

"Whoa, whoa, whoa. He's a special type of man," Lacey interjects her misconception.

CONFIDENT SENSUALITY

Candace places her hand on Lacey's thigh. "Special? How?"

"For starters, if she"—she points to me—"shows him any form of emotion, he's going to feel like he's won something. It's an ego trip for him, so she's not letting him off the hook by not showing emotion. She's putting him on it, making him uncomfortable."

Candace nods, then glances at me. "How do you feel about all of this?"

"I'm nervous. It's not like I was expecting him to profess his undying love for me. I just…I don't know…We had sex. My emotions have already betrayed me, so I'm not sure if I can go back in there and pretend that I wasn't affected."

Lacey puts her forehead in her hand. "Bitch, practice makes perfect. Get through a day or two, and you're good until he cracks."

"He won't crack." I'm certain of it.

Lacey and Candace laugh.

"You'll have to excuse her," Lacey explains on my behalf. "She's only been with one guy. And even with that being said, he was a child, so…" She shrugs.

"As I was saying, I don't know how I'm going to emotionally remove myself."

"You have to think about how angry he made you. Maybe start looking at him in a more negative light." Candace doesn't fully understand what's going on. As far as she knows, we're just trying to manipulate him into wanting me, which I guess we are but for much, much deeper and perhaps more cynical reasons that Candace may think.

"I don't know," she continues. "I just feel like you need to be completely emotionally removed to get the attention of someone as stubborn and prideful as him."

She's so right. I nod.

"You've got this."

I nod again, because I don't think I do. They know it too.

We go through my bag of clothes again, deciding when I'm going to wear what and with what.

Chapter Thirteen

Angelo

I haven't slept a wink, which is nothing new, considering I've suffered from insomnia my entire adult life. It's now 5:00 a.m., and I've managed to read an entire book, watch a couple of episodes of *Law & Order*, shower, shave, iron my clothes, have breakfast, and get dressed for work. I live in a decent home in Providence, Rhode Island. And by decent, I mean a three-story, six-bedroom, four-and-a half-bathroom home.

I have another home in Martha's Vineyard, a charming town in Massachusetts, where it almost always snows during this time of year. Very few know of that home; it's where I go to completely isolate.

I know what you may be wondering: why do I, one person, own so much space? Because I bought these homes for my family. The family that was ripped away from me by Lisa Baldeo. She will soon know what it's like to have something so precious ripped away from you.

Today, I have to address the misconduct that took place between Melissa and me, which means I'm going to have to deal with more attitude, more back talk, and more pushing for information. I could just end her life now and spare myself, but there is no fun in that. I want Lisa to writhe in discomfort and watch front row as I take her child away from her in every aspect of the term *take*. She (Lisa) will be showing up to Rhode Island soon, I'm sure. And she will think she has everything figured out, but she is most certainly in for a rude awakening.

I get to work at exactly 6:30 a.m. I am fully aware that Melissa will be late, and I will not tolerate—

"Good morning," a familiar voice greets me.

It's Melissa, standing at my desk with two files in her left hand and what I presume is coffee in the other hand. Sampson must have let her in. *Fucking kiss-ass.*

"I spoke with the detective that is currently on the drug bust case, Detective Layard."

She's wearing a leather pencil leather skirt that stops just above the knees with a crisp white blouse.

"We were looking at the security cameras from the location that everything took place. He and I both agree that something doesn't seem right."

Her mane is pulled into a high bun, accentuating her cheekbones.

"He tells me you guys have been following this case for months, which leads me to believe that this whole thing is game."

"A game?" I ask, not really paying attention.

"Yes. Whoever the mastermind is behind this, they wanted to be caught. They wanted to be seen. It appears as if they've been meticulous in calculating their moves specifically to not get caught, up until this point, that is. But now, everything seems a bit too easy. Therefore, at this point, I think they're just setting us up. Or trying to, at least."

"Hmph." She's wearing nude pumps so her legs look endless and heavenly.

She turns around to place the file on my desk and open it up. She continues to state her hunches, which are all correct, but goddamn, her ass sits up so plump and voluminous.

"Moving forward, I don't believe we should give any indication that we're on to them. I believe we should go about this like every other case of this nature. They're watching our every move, just as we are watching theirs."

My eyes meet hers. Did she even notice me ogling her? I'm sure she did. I haven't even moved from my spot at the door. Why hasn't she made a smart remark about it yet?

I move further into my office and close my door. I start walking toward her slowly, looking for her pulse in her throat to quicken or those hazel eyes to darken or her breathing to pick up.

Nothing.

What are you hiding, Melissa?

"I would like to go to the actual crime scene with whomever is assigned to go so I can gather evidence or at least learn how to do so and see what the process is.

"Not yet."

I'm expecting attitude, maybe a smart and/or witty remark, but I'm met with…compliance?

"Okay. What am I doing here at the office today?"

I stare at her.

"Also where can I go for lunch around here? I forgot my packed lunch at home." She shakes her head at herself.

CONFIDENT SENSUALITY

I give her a few options and tell her about the courtyard in our facility where she can eat her lunch.

"Thanks. I'll take it at noon today because I want to be back in time for when Detective Layard comes up at 1:00 p.m. to discuss his findings and our proposed next steps."

I offer her a curt nod and then pull out the chair, gesturing for her to have a seat. I then tell her what her responsibilities for today are, which is essentially just reviewing old cases. I am expecting kickback with this as well.

Nothing. I get nothing.

In fact, her demeanor is awfully cold. Almost dismissive. I'm sure this newfound demeanor is associated with our sexual encounter.

Stacy walks in, stating that her lunch hour is free today, so she can come discuss a few cases with me.

I glance at Melissa for one of her snappy responses.

Not a word. She appears to be enthralled with the new case.

I politely decline Stacy's offer.

"But we haven't been able to go over very much since you began your mentorship with her."

This is it, I thought. Melissa is definitely going to say something full of wit and attitude now.

"Stacy," she starts, "you and I have known of each other long enough for you to remember my name." She sounds bored. I'm almost disappointed.

She ignores Melissa and continues pouting in my direction, which is exceptionally juvenile. "Stacy, this conversation is over."

She makes a rather elaborate exit.

I await a comment from Melissa from what just transpired.

Nada.

"Is there…" I clear my throat. "Is there something you'd like to discuss?"

She looks at me and squints, as if she's thinking, and finally says, "How long is my lunch today? I may actually be able to drive home and pick it up."

I stare at her again. "Uh, you can just take the hour."

She smiles. "Perfect."

Her dimples are quite deep. And her perfect white teeth in contrast with her dark lipstick and chocolate skin is not a fair combination in the midst of everything going on.

She is testing me. She must be. She is fully aware of her features.

I excuse myself to go get the cases for she and me to discuss.

She nods without even looking up at me.

I'm gone for a total of five minutes, if even that. And I come back to Sampson leaning on my desk engaged in banter with Melissa. She's sitting with her back to me. He's standing facing her, not acknowledging my presence.

She is laughing.

At him.

With him.

Her head tilts back in a bout of more laughter so her neck is exposed, and Sampson's eyes instinctively goes to that delicate skin.

She thinks this is a fucking game. "Sampson, you can go." My voice is curt. Not angry. Curt. For the record, however, I am very angry.

He looks up at me. Melissa sets her pen down. Laughter comes to an end. I sincerely hope that he does not make me say it again.

He says his good-byes to Melissa and brushes past me.

A silent warning.

I close my door behind him and find my seat at my desk. Melissa does not make eye contact but glances up at the clock. "Jesus. It's only seven, and I'm already starving."

"You should not make a habit of leading men on." This is it. She's going to lose her shit right now.

"What gives you the impression that I'm leading men on?"

Correction: *I'm* going to lose my shit. "Your interactions with Sampson are indicative that you are interested in more than a friendship."

"Okay."

Okay? O-fucking-kay? "What you're saying is… is that you're interested in Sampson?"

"I haven't said that." Boredom. She meets my incredulousness with boredom.

"What are you saying?" I ask.

"What are you asking?" She still hasn't looked at me.

"I'm just saying that it appears as if you're flirting with Sampson with no true intention based on my observation."

"Hmph."

What the fuck?

"Is that the case?" I ask. If that is the case, that would be unprofessional.

"It is not." She is still looking over the initial case from this morning, taking notes.

"Right. Does he know that?" I need to know so that I do not have to deal with another misconduct situation. I'm sure she knows that, which reminds me…

"Professor Angelo," she starts.

Professor?

"Sampson and I," she continues, "are adults capable of having a conversation without misunderstanding the motives. However, thank you for your concern."

"I beg to differ. I acknowledge that you're an adult, but men are a different ball game. They see and/or hear whatever they want to. I suggest making it clear that you are not interested intimately."

"Thank you. If I see fit for that conversation to take place, I will take that advice."

What am I supposed to say to that? I cannot press the issue because of how ridiculous that will make me look.

The morning goes by with the two of us discussing and reviewing old cases. She took note of the points I told her to look out for and asked me appropriate questions. I gave her some homework and suggested books for her to read to gain a better understanding of what we deal with on a daily basis.

"Forensics can be tricky in the sense that you have to be able to remove yourself to be able to get into the mind of the accused." I recall briefly having mentioned this in the past. "Think things through the way the person who committed the crime would have thought it through. In other words, you have to study the people involved more than the actual case. Details are incredibly important."

She nods, still taking notes. Not making eye contact.

I know what this is about.

I have to say something.

She's not mad.

She's…indifferent.

I'm not sure at this time if I'm able to determine which one is better.

She glances up at the clock. "Ugh. Thank God. I'm so hungry today." She sets her pen down. "Can I take this with me?" She points to one of the cases we were reviewing.

"Yes, but be mindful. Do not lose and/or forget it."

She smiles nicely, not mischievously. "I won't." She gathers her belongings, grabbing her jacket off the back of her chair, and bids me a farewell until later. "I'll be back in time for when Detective Layard comes up."

"Sounds good."

CONFIDENT SENSUALITY

She saunters out, and Sampson glides in. *For fuck's sake.*

"Hey, Professor Angelo. I'm working on my final project. I just had a quick question for you: how did your knowledge with of bloodstain pattern analysis..."

I'm not listening. I'm watching Melissa walk over to the elevator because her hips are swaying just a little bit more today.

"Did you hear me?" He follows my line of vision. "Ah, I see."

If looks could kill.

He puts his hands up in an "I come in piece" manner. "Look, Melissa is a great person. Really down to earth. So it's clear as day that you've made it to her shit list. And I'm sure that being on the receiving end of that is a less-than-desirable feeling."

"So she's angry." I can deal with anger. I can play with anger. I can manipulate anger. Anger prevents logic from having its way with a situation.

"Nah, she's not angry. Not by any means. She's sort of...done. Removed. I don't know what you did, but I'd rather her just be angry."

What the fuck do you *know about Melissa?*

"Anyways, I'll just go ask one of the other mentors my question."

They're communicating outside of work. That has to be the case for him to be so sure of his words where Melissa is concerned. He still doesn't know her that well. Not as well as I do. His words hold little to no merit.

I shake my head.

I've been studying this woman for years. Her and her family. I know what I am up against. She has this alluring aura, an infectious smile, and a contagious laugh. But her fight is unimaginable; she just won't give. This has to be her expressing her anger, but she can't derail my plan.

The only time she's at her most vulnerable is when I'm touching her. I have to get her back to that moment we had when we were having sex. I'm taking everything—all of it, with no apologies. I need an avenue to get back into her pretty little head so I can convince her that I am giving piece of myself to her. She needs to believe that I have her somewhere special in my heart so she can willingly offer herself to me.

Melissa

I know I left my lunch on the table. However, my table is empty. Maybe Lacey put it in the fridge.

I walk over to the fridge, grabbing the handle, when there's a knock at my door. I pause, with my hand on the fridge. Lacey is at work, and Candace is at work. And even if Candace was off, she knows that Lacey is at work, which leaves me with…no one. Also, neither of the two would knock. This would not be as concerning as it currently is if I didn't just leave the office of a man plotting the ruin of me and/or my family right under my nose.

I turn around slowly, staring in the direction of the door.

Maybe they'll leave.

Knock, knock.

Nope. Whoever that is, they're either hopeful or persistent, or they saw me come in. With the way my life has been going, it is more likely that I am being watched. Over the past few weeks, the unbelievable has become more believable.

I turn around and do a quick survey of my surroundings, spotting the pots and pans on the kitchen counter, Lacey's generously sized textbooks on our couch, and the broom leaning up against our balcony door, which sits right behind our couch.

I have options. These options are, of course, available if this individual makes it past my threshold.

Knock, knock, knock.

Yes, I am going to answer the door.

What choice do I have? They are clearly not going away, and I just have this hunch, for lack of a better word, that the police would make nothing better. I may be overanalyzing, but I doubt it. Nothing has been as it seems lately.

I will not be running away from this. I cannot. What good would that do me? Prove to myself and whoever is at that door that I simply came into this world to exist? I think not. I am a badass.

I am answering that damn door.

Knock, knock, knock.

I walk over to the door, look through the peephole, and see a man who looks very similar to Angelo. With a buzz cut.

Hmm.

I turn the knob. "Can I help you?"

He holds a significant portion of Angelo's features. His jawline is not an angular work of art like Angelo's, but his eyes hold the same shade of striking green. His nose doesn't have that extra feature that alludes to a previous fracture, perhaps multiple. He has more of a gentle and polished finish to his features, like perhaps he hasn't seen as much turmoil as poor Angelo.

CONFIDENT SENSUALITY

But let's go back to his eyes. They're enticing, yes, but am I enticed? No. Truth is, he holds my attention, for I believe that no matter what comes out of his mouth, his eyes will tell me more. They're rather piercing. The little cilia that sit on my nerve endings are standing at attention, but I'm staring back with no fear.

He's definitely related to Angelo.

He tilts his head. "My brother did well." Wow. He revealed that piece of information quickly. This man doesn't appear threatening. Just sneaky.

"That depends."

"On?"

"Who your brother is."

He laughs. "You know my brother *very* well, Bella." I don't know how much he really knows. The way he's presenting himself tells me he'd like me to *think* that he holds a declamatory amount of information that could potentially make or break me. He's convincing, yes, but am I convinced? No. If this internship taught me anything, I learned to disrobe myself of my personality and morals and step into the mind of a manipulator. If I learn something new about them willingly, I've stumbled upon an honest person. If I have to manipulate them myself to get information, then I've embarked on a game of push and pull.

May the best criminal win.

"Well, for starters, my name is Melissa."

He nods. "Melissa, you are quite the distraction."

I shrug. "I try."

He steps a little closer. "Uh-uh. I don't recall inviting you in."

He steps back and nods. "I suppose you're correct." All right, so he's definitely no real threat. Either that or he's afraid of what Angelo will do to him if he does anything to me.

"So what can I help you with?"

"I don't think I'm the one that needs help, love."

"Melissa. My name is Melissa."

"Well, Melissa. I suppose we should start with who my brother is, yes?"

"Sure."

"He has placed you in a great deal of danger, my dear." That tells me nothing about who his brother is, but I can't acknowledge that I'm on to him. I think I'm doing pretty damn good, if I do say so myself. The goal is to reveal nothing. Do I know exactly what he's talking about? Absolutely. Am I going to show it? I'll be damned.

"Is that right?"

He gives a short humorless laugh. "Melissa, do you have any idea who my brother is?"

"No." I say this slowly to emphasize just how much air I believe is circulating in his skull, taking the place of his brain. "I thought we established this."

He's asking me questions because he does not want to reveal how little he knows. In other words, he wants to know what I know. This man is not here to help me. He's here because he's looking for Angelo, and somehow, he believes that there is a connection between him and me, which I suppose there is, but how does he know? Where is his source of information? If he came here to me, Angelo most certainly didn't tell him. This isn't Angelo's doing. It's very sloppy and rather juvenile.

"Lorenzo Marcel Angelo."

Just his name gives me goose bumps. "Why is it that you're so adamant on making me aware of your absentee brother? I don't even know your name, yet you seem interested in devoting a conversation to a man only one of us knows. Why didn't you just bring him here to introduce us? I'm sure he's just as charming as you." I'll ask questions to express interest. For the record, I am not interested because I am aware. Probably more aware than this guy.

"No, I'm afraid he falls short."

I almost laughed. Almost. "Hmm. Bummer. So what's your name?"

"Donatello."

I stick my hand out to shake his, never breaking eye contact. "It's nice to meet you."

He blesses me with a humorous smirk. "Likewise."

"So is that it? You just wanted to tell me that I'm in danger of this Lorenzo Marcel, is it?"

"You don't seem concerned."

It's my turn to dish out a humorless laugh. "Donatello," I admonish him, "you don't know me as well as you may think."

"Is that right?"

"Absolutely."

"And how do you propose I get to know you?"

"I would never propose such a thing for then you, my new friend, would be in a great deal of danger." I repeat his words to him to indicate that I've been paying attention and that because of my focus, it's not likely that he stands a chance in wining whatever it is we just agreed to play. "We just can't have that, can we?"

He may very well stand a chance, but if I convince him that he doesn't in a decent enough manner, he will likely just throw in the towel and abandon an opportunity to explore what his chances are at defeating me.

He does just that: he nods in defeat. "Hmm. I see it. I see what my brother sees in you, and I respect it, which is rare. All I came to say is watch your back."

"My eyes are wide open. I'm watching everything."

He places his hands in his pockets and steps back off my threshold. "You have a pleasant afternoon, Melissa."

"You do the same, love."

I shut my door and lock it, letting out a gust of wind that was threatening to form a hurricane in my chest.

Lisa

We—Donatello, Ramona, and I—are sitting in my rental car, watching her walk out to her car.

"Where is she going?" I whisper more to myself. But of course, Donatello had to respond.

"I don't know, Lisa." He sounds rather exasperated with me. I was fine on my own. He said he wanted to learn the ropes and take his brother down. We've worked well before, but his impatience is laying on my nerves. If he keeps this up, I'll have to get rid of him. He's risking the unfolding of a well thought out and long overdue plan.

"She's likely just going back to work," Ramona cuts in. Her tone has been a bit softer toward Donatello. Their method of communication has always been rather abrasive. They never seemed to be able to communicate without firing insults at one another.

"Listen, children." I cut in. "I told you two the plan. It is going to take time. We cannot just dive in like idiots. I have been doing this for a very long time. Just relax, okay?"

"I'm relaxed," he says, mumbling in Italian.

Ramona stays silent.

I roll my eyes and shake my head. "Focus," I say while watching her climb into her vehicle. "What did she say when you went up there?"

He sighs, and I swear to God, if he does that shit one more time, I will put a bullet in his skull.

"Why exactly didn't you just go up there and claim your kid?" Donatello questions.

I pick up the heavy piece of steel from my lap and point it in his direction. "Because, you impotent dumbass, I'm not supposed to be here in this fucking state. I live in Maryland, remember?"

Ramona lays her hand on my wrist, prompting the lowering of my gun.

He puts his hands up in surrender. "Okay, okay."

I set my weapon of choice back down on my lap, giving in to my niece's efforts to instill peace amongst us. "Now will you please tell me what she said?" It is not a question. I am just being polite.

He hesitates, then says, "Do you have any idea who she is?"

"I've been trying to tell her," Ramona chimes in.

I furrow my brows. "What does that mean?"

He shakes his head in a somber manner. "Lisa, I'm asking you. Do you even know who your daughter is?"

What kind of question is that? "Of course, I do. She is my kid."

I catch a glimpse of Ramona rolling her eyes in the rearview mirror.

"Those tactics that you gave me to get her to succumb to me? They failed." Donatello shakes his head, portraying his lack of faith in me once more.

"Obviously. You're here, and she is not. You must've done something wrong. What did you tell her?"

"Exactly what you said," he stated with exasperation.

"I'm sensing some tension. So bring that down a bit please, and thanks."

He gives me a feigned look of indifference.

"First of all," I continue, "if you would've stressed what kind of person Lorenzo is, like I told you, she would have bought it. Did you mention me like I said? Did you say that he did terrible things to me?"

"I didn't even make it that far. She wouldn't let me. She had tactics of her own, like she knew I was coming."

"I told you this, Mother," Ramona states.

I shake my head with impatience, trying to silence everyone. "That doesn't even make any sense."

"Lisa, this girl is too smart for your own good."

"My own good? Excuse me?" I don't particularly like to be questioned.

"Melissa didn't even give me a chance to convince her that she's in danger. She answered me rather confidently. She's not worried about my brother at all. I think she might have feelings for him."

I shake my head. "Nope. You're wrong. She's just manipulating him, like I taught her to do."

CONFIDENT SENSUALITY

"You're delusional."

"Ramona, I swear to God. Not another word."

She plops back in her seat.

Donatello stares at me incredulously. "Wanna know what she told me?" He asks, leaning forward as if to emphasize his point. "She said that if she came with me, I would be in danger. She basically told me that she's in charge of this whole fucking operation. She showed not an ounce of fear. The bitch didn't even blink an eye when she opened the door and learned that I wasn't Lorenzo."

"First of all, my child is no bitch. Second of all, if you had just stuck with the plan, Melissa would have been with us. Or you, at least. Until I pretended to be hurt so that she could demand that you bring her to me."

He scoffs, "You are delusional. You and I are referring to two completely different women. And for someone who boasts about her child, you know very little about her."

"Look, our approach in this was a bit...childish, for lack of a better word," I say, dismissing his last statement. I know my child very well. "Because I wasn't sure what you were made of, Donatello. And to be quite frank, you haven't shown me much of anything," I say, giving him a pointed look. "And we're behind. She's likely going on a date with him and will return in a few short hours. And at that time, I will go up there and put on a show. She'll surely come with me."

"How do you know they're going on a date?" He asks me this not because he wants my honest answer but because he doubts my theory. He is challenging me, and I am not happy about it.

"Because she is my child. I know her."

I stare at him.

He stares back.

"What?" I shout.

He shakes his head.

"I'm telling you, she's giving him a run for his money." I know what I'm saying.

"You know? Melissa might very well be your blind spot. It's crazy because when I last saw you, you had the all-seeing eye. Now that you've placed your only child in the cross fire, you have no idea how to act."

I put my binoculars down. "Really? I don't know how to act? And you couldn't carry out the only job I gave you."

He sighs, ignoring me. "Let me take it from here."

I roll my eyes at him, but he continues, "I can tell you one thing: they are most definitely not going on a date. She told me she didn't know Lorenzo. She's obviously protecting him. She knows more than you think. Why would someone protect another individual without even knowing what they're protecting them from? Why would she risk so much for a man that you claim she's manipulating?"

I squint my eyes in both suspicion and confusion. "All right, Donatello. What's your plan then?"

Ramona

He kisses me like I am his last breath.

It is addicting.

He grabs my hips, grinding into me, so a moan escapes my lips.

"Sshh. She'll hear us," Donatello whispers.

We've driven back to a hotel because Mother felt we needed a full night's rest to carry out this new elaborate plan that Donatello proposed.

"Should we go back to your room then?" I ask. Mother and I are only separated by a door.

"Nah. Just don't scream. You know how crazy we can get."

He picks me up and tosses me on the bed, and I let out an excited yelp.

He laughs. "Maybe we should go back to my room."

He picks me up and carries me down the hall several doors down from Mother's.

We get to his room, and he rips off my clothes and kisses me everywhere. I love it when he loses control like this. I've actually grown to love everything about him, but mostly his lips.

On our first time, which was also my first time, I just wanted to keep kissing him because I was immediately obsessed with his lips. They're soft. They're plush. They match mine. We're perfect together.

He flings me on his bed and starts ripping his own clothes off. I love watching. His body is manly; he's built like a football player with a broad chest and boulders for shoulders.

He prowls for me, and I get excited all over again. He grabs my leg and pulls me toward him. My yelp is louder and more carefree this time because I have no one to hide from.

"You are so fucking gorgeous," he says against my neck, plunging his fingers into me.

CONFIDENT SENSUALITY

My back arches, and my breathing increases. I grab his length and guide him toward my entrance. I turn my face toward his lips and start to kiss him, and he slams into me.

We make love multiple times into the early morning. Wild, crazy love.

*****

I get up at 3:00 a.m., get dressed, and kiss him on the lips softly so I don't wake him. "Until next time, my love."

Chapter Fourteen

Melissa

Should I tell him?

I should tell him, right?

Will he believe me?

Why wouldn't he?

Donatello does not strike me as threatening or powerful, but he does have access to information. He knows where I live. He knows that I withheld information about Angelo. He knew to come to me, so he is certain about his knowledge of my connection to Angelo.

What the fuck did I get myself into?

I call Lacey. "Yo," she answers quickly, likely on her lunch break as well.

I fill her in. "Maybe you should stay with Candace for a bit."

"Duly noted, but where are you gonna stay?"

Fuck. "Fantastic question." We can't both stay with Candace because Candace still lives with her family. She can't very well have the two of us stay at her place indefinitely. Her family is well aware of her sexuality and has met Lacey and welcomes her with open arms. However, my random extended presence will not only put them in danger but raise a heap of questions and concerns.

"Put your big girl panties on and ask Angelo's bitch ass."

"What? No. I cannot do that. He's the reason I'm in this mess."

"Exactly why he's going to be the one to get you out of it. Donatello came to you, hoping you'd reveal something about Angelo, which means Angelo's better at hiding than you."

"But, Lacey, I—"

"What are your options? Are you going to call dear ol' Mommy?"

I don't answer.

"Do it. Ask her for some money for a hotel, and there's no way she'll give you the third degree."

I sigh. "I'll let you know how this conversation goes."

"Wait, which one? Do not call your mother. I was being sarcastic."

"No, no. I'm going back in to talk to Angelo about everything."

"Please do."

"Don't go to the apartment alone tonight."

"Got it."

My appetite has dwindled down to nerves, so I waltzed back into his office with my untouched lunch and fifteen minutes to spare before Detective Layard comes up.

He looks up at me. "Did you enjoy your lunch?"

"No."

He squints his eyes at me, leaning back in his chair. "What happened?"

"Who's Donatello?"

He takes his glasses off and stands. "Why are you asking me that question?"

"Because he came to my fucking home." I take some deep breaths, set my lunch down on his desk, and take a sip of his water.

"What did he say?" He's on alert yet still calm.

"He…" Can I trust Angelo? Can I trust Donatello? No. I definitely cannot trust Donatello. Lacey's words bounce around in my skull. Right now, Angelo is literally all I have. "He wanted me to know that I was in great danger because of you."

He puts his hands in his pockets. His nostrils flare, and his jaw clenches. "What did you say?"

"I said I didn't know you."

CONFIDENT SENSUALITY

His eyes, for the first time since I've known this man, is expressive. They show surprise. "What else did you say?"

I shrug. "I said 'Thanks for the warning, but I don't need it.'"

I can't quite place his reaction. "Why?"

I am going to flip this fucking desk. "What do you mean why?"

"What is your motive? Why not just tell him you know me and point him in my direction? Why not just run to his rescue?"

I squint my eyes at him. "Have you been drinking?"

He opens his mouth to respond, but I cut him off. "Angelo, I have never seen that man before today. I know nothing about him, yet he knows that you and I know one another, or at least he wanted me to believe that. Why would I side with a man I do not know? What"—I shake my head—"who do you think I am?"

He stares at me. The silence stretches for God knows how long. "I just expected that you would take the first avenue to your freedom. It's human nature."

"You're right, but that was not an avenue to freedom. Therefore, I did not take it. Donatello's approach was very..." I'm searching for the correct word.

"Amateur."

"Yes. It was clear that he only knew as much as his source fed him."

He nods. He knows more, but he won't tell me right now. Because despite the fact that I proved some semblance of loyalty, it wasn't necessarily direct loyalty to him. It was just a matter of utilizing the knowledge I was blessed with. In other words, all I've proven was my loyalty to myself, and he benefitted.

"So," I continue, "I cannot go back to that apartment tonight."

"Right."

What do I say? Fuck. "You are likely more aware of your brother's next move than I am. What do you suggest?" That wasn't exactly what I wanted to ask, but it's better than nothing.

He picks up his phone. "Sampson, Detective Layard is scheduled to be here in less than five minutes. Please stand in for me and report back to me with details on my work line later this evening. Be sure to reschedule my remaining meetings for next week. I have to step away for the remainder of the afternoon."

CONFIDENT SENSUALITY

He hangs up.

Ugh. I really wanted to be a part of that case. I must be showing my disappointment because Angelo orders me to "Stop pouting."

"I am not pouting."

He smirks. "Sure."

Whatever.

"Grab your things. We're heading out."

We're? I'm not even going to ask any questions. Honestly, in the grand scheme of things, this is likely my best next move.

We leave via the back door, a back door that I was not introduced to during my orientation and one I am therefore completely unaware of. However, at this point, that's neither here nor there. I follow him down a flight of stairs, which leads to a dimly lit parking garage.

Where there is only one car parked.

His car. Well, his truck. It's a Ford F-150.

He's moving with purpose, but not fear. That makes one of us. I mean there is purpose in my steps as well, just with the added element of fear.

I look over my shoulder, assessing my surroundings, wondering which way is out. Then questioning if this is how I die. Maybe this was all a setup.

Maybe he knew I wasn't going to give in to his brother.

Oh God.

I am going to die.

This is it.

I should've called my mom.

"Get in." He's holding the passenger door open for me.

"How do I know this wasn't a setup?"

He steps closer to me. "If this was a setup, you think you'd be able to get away, Melissa?"

Fuck. Good point. However, my point is that he's not saying anything to me. I don't know where I'm going or what we're doing. How do you expect me to not think this is a setup? "Well then, can you please tell me the plan, Lorenzo?"

His eyes are alight with anger. *Well, well, well.* If it isn't emotion breaking free. I know. Poor timing, but I almost want to pat myself on the back.

"Get in the fucking car," he fumes.

"Okay, okay, okay." I literally have zero other options.

He walks around to the passenger side and starts the car, and we're moving. As we emerge from the secret private parking dungeon, the silence thickens

CONFIDENT SENSUALITY

the tension. I'm not sure if it has to do with me or if he's thinking.

Should I say something?

What would I even say?

I settle for eating my lunch.

I spill some of my soda on his cup holder.

He shakes his head. "Fucking child."

"Fuck you. You mean to tell me you've never spilled anything?"

He sighs. "This is going to be a long drive."

I take a bite of my sandwich. "It sure is," I say through a mouthful.

*****

The drive is long indeed.

We bicker about my seat belt, the crumbs that were spilling from my sandwich, my bag of chips, and the grapes that fell out of my bowl when we hit a bump in the road, and all of a sudden, the length of my skirt becomes an issue.

"That skirt is incredibly too short."

I take my time to finish chewing and swallowing my grapes, because here's how I see it: he's only bringing this up now because I am a lot more verbal than I was at the office this morning. I am clearly not as emotionally removed. However, a random man showing up at your door with strange intentions will provoke those suppressed emotions. He's taking advantage of what appears to be a window of opportunity to him. I'm interacting with him more, so I think that he's using this time to say what he's wanted to say since this morning.

"What you meant to say is that I'm wearing this skirt very well."

He looks at me and shakes his head. "Despite the fact that the skirt is being worn well, it was still not professional for work."

"Why are you addressing this now?"

"Because I did not address it earlier."

"Right. And now is a better time to address it as opposed to earlier?"

He does not answer me.

"You know what I don't understand?" I challenge. "Your incessant need to be the one with the last word. It's absurd to you that you could be wrong. That maybe there is another perspective. For someone so intelligent, you have a very narrow view on just about everything."

I pop another few grapes in my mouth and chew violently, causing me to bite my tongue. "Fuck."

CONFIDENT SENSUALITY

He looks over at me as I swallow the half-chewed grapes. I pull down the mirror in his visor and examine my poor tongue as blood drips onto my skirt.

I let out a whimper.

Closing the visor and returning my tongue to my mouth, I glimpse over at him. "Thee whath you thid?" That was supposed to sound like "see what you did," but half of my tongue is numb and throbbing.

He laughs.

He fucking laughs. And it's genuine, because his eyes crinkle at the corners and it holds a heavy, sort of carefree, gut-derived tone.

I love it.

I stared for a bit.

When he catches me staring, I cross my arms and look ahead at the road. The rest of the ride is met with my pouting and, of course, his silence. Occasionally, he'd spare me some glimpses, but that's about it.

*****

We stop off at an elaborate outlet.

"This could be dangerous," I comment. "What are we here for?"

"You."

I angle my entire body toward him, tilting my head. "Please elaborate."

"You need clothes."

"Jesus, you hate the skirt that much?"

He rolls his eyes. "No. We'll be out here for a bit, and you don't have any clothes."

I let the words sink in. Correct me if I'm wrong, but kidnappers don't usually allow their victim to go shopping. However, the words "we'll be out here for a bit" gives a completely different indication.

"Stop overthinking. We need to go in hiding for a bit. You need somethings to wear while we're out here. Simple as that."

Ah, very true. "I'm skeptical. Sue me."

He just stares at me.

"Let's just go," I demand.

We get to our first store, Pink. My choice. They have cute sleepwear, so I pick up a few things, already realizing that I'm going to have to use mom's emergency credit card because my bank account isn't going to be able to handle another wardrobe makeover.

CONFIDENT SENSUALITY

Angelo follows close behind with his hands in his pockets. We get up to the register, and I begin to pull out my wallet when the cashier tells me my total of 177.80. However, Angelo beats me to the punch, inserting his card and grabbing my bag of merchandise.

We walk out the store, and he says, "You need boots and real clothes, Melissa."

"I'm not a child, Angelo. I know that."

I glimpse over at Victoria's Secret, thinking about my initial plan.

I can't seduce him, can I? Maybe I should've gotten sexier sleepwear. I need to go to Victoria's Secret.

"Okay, you know what?" His impatience is rearing its ugly head. "You go get the clothes, and I'll go get your boots. What's your size?"

"Ten."

He looks me up and down. "Wow. You have big feet."

My jaw drops. "You are so fucking rude." I raise my hand to swat his chest, but he catches my wrist and pulls me close to him. "You have one hour. We meet here in one hour, Melissa." He pulls me closer. "And don't even think about running. I will find you."

I smirk, leaning in to graze my lips over his. "So this is a kidnap."

He lets go of me, shaking his head and pulling out his wallet, giving me his card. "One hour."

"I got it."

I start walking away, running through a number of possibilities, replaying the events of today over and over, finally concluding that I am batshit insane. Because I suppose this time is as good as any to run, correct? The issue is that I do not want to run, and I'm not certain I can tell you why. In fact, to add insult to injury, I am getting semi excited about this shopping spree, and yes, even more excited about getting this sexy sleepwear, maybe even some lingerie. This would be the perfect time to get back to the plan. We're going to be alone. I have to do something.

This obviously wasn't a part of his plan. His brother threw a wrench in this whole operation, and it is so abundantly clear that he wasn't expecting me to respond the way I did.

Things have most definitely changed.

I have to call Lacey.

I reach for my phone in my purse. It's not there. *He didn't.*

CONFIDENT SENSUALITY

I turn around to see if he's still at the same spot that I left him. And what do you know? He's standing there, waving my phone at me. Smiling.

Welp. Things haven't changed that much.

I flip him off, shake my head, and turn around, heading to my original destination, hoping I'm able to carry out this desperate plan of mine.

*****

One hour and fifteen minutes later, I am on my way to meet an impatient Angelo at our designated spot. I'm pretty satisfied with my purchases. My hands are full with bags because my purchases were on Angelo's dime. Granted, shopping is a weakness of mine with or without Angelo's funds.

Walking over to him, I take in his athletic build, his broad shoulders, and thick mane.

He is quite the specimen.

"You're late."

"What? Did you just go buy a couple of things and then wait here for an hour?"

"You're late," he repeats.

"I'm aware."

He's holding two bags.

"What's that?" I ask.

"You'll find out later. We've been here for too long."

"What do you mean?"

"We need to stick to the schedule, Melissa."

He reaches for some of my bags and shakes his head with a smirk. "Victoria's Secret?" And just like that, he's a different man. This man is much easier to handle.

I smile. "Yes."

"What's in the bag?" He peeks.

I swat his hand. "You'll find out later. We've been here for too long," I repeat his words to him.

His smirk remains intact. "Later," he confirms. "Okay."

We get back to his truck, he loads the bags, and we're on the road again. Soon enough, we're in line to get on a ferry. "A ferry?" I ask.

He nods. "Yes, Melissa. This is called a ferry."

I squint at him. "I realize that. But damn. Where are we going? You're really trying to get away."

"Not get away. Just get far enough to buy time."

"Time for what?"

"You'll see."

Oh, for fuck's sake.

CONFIDENT SENSUALITY

"Well, I need to know something, Angelo. You can't spoon-feed me. Despite what you may think, I am a grown woman. I can handle it. I need time to prepare for whatever the fuck is coming too."

"I am preparing. You don't need to prepare for anything."

What the fuck does that mean? "So I'm just here for what? Decoration?"

He doesn't answer me.

The rest of the journey is met with silence. I'm not going to beg him to put me in the loop. I'm just going to do my own thing.

One nap later, we are pulling up to a charmingly beautiful cabin. Snow has begun to fall, making my surroundings look very picturesque.

"We're here," he says, removing his key and getting out of the truck. I'm a little sluggish after my nap, so my movements are delayed, but Angelo makes it to my side, opening my door, with the bags already in his left hand, reaching out to me with his right.

"Come on," he coaxes.

I take his hand, hopping out, and of course, the minute my feet connect with the ground, I slip on the thin layer of snow that coats it. He catches me, dropping the bags.

"Jesus, Melissa. Are you okay?"

"Yeah, just a little groggy."

He steadies me, then he lets go of me momentarily. After he retrieves the bags off the floor, he notices that an item fell out, and what do you know? It's one of the laced numbers I bought from Victoria's Secret.

He reached for it slowly, holding it between his two fingers. He then looks at me with untamed desire. He grabs my hand, walks us to the front door of the cobblestone cabin, and opens it up.

He sets everything down, except my lingerie. He opens it out to get a better look. I gaze around at the rustic wooden and stone interior. It looks like a home, yet it doesn't appear to have been lived in. The fireplace is made of stone. There are floor to ceiling windows overlooking a lake, cathedral ceilings, and lights in the shape of candle hanging from said ceiling.

The stairs are off to my left, and they spiral to a balcony on the second floor. I am in awe. I look back over to Angelo. He's already staring at me.

"This is amazing, Angelo."

He doesn't answer me, so now we stand in the foyer, staring at one another. His chest rises and falls with purpose, almost as if he's trying to control his breathing.

Should I do something?

I take a step toward him. He licks his lips and then looks at mine. I take another step, so now I am breathing his air.

"Do you want a kiss, Angelo?"

He nods.

I put my hands on both sides of his face and graze my lips over his, teasing. He doesn't like that, but I love what it does to him. I feel powerful.

He grabs my hips and devours my lips, backing me into the door. He hikes my legs up around his waist. And just like that, I'm lost in this man, completely consumed by the way he's devouring my lips and grinding into my core.

I lace my fingers through his hair, and he groans through the kiss into my mouth. He rips my blouse off.

That shit was expensive.

He then sets my legs down, steps back, and examines my leather skirt. As he starts shaking his head, he kneels and starts unzipping it.

"This fucking skirt," he mumbles. "I absolutely hate it."

I let out a breathless laugh. "No, you don't. You love it. I wore it for you."

He looks up at me, pulling my skirt off and demanding that I step out of it. Picking up my lingerie, he stands, hands it to me, and says, "Wear this for me."

"Where is the bathroom?"

He shakes his head. "Do it right here. Put it on in front of me."

I remove my bra and underwear and start slipping into the one-piece, crotchless, lace front, with a deep V-shaped neckline. Once I have it on in its entirety, not that there's much to put on, I look over at him. And he stands there without moving. He looks me up and down.

"Turn around," he says in a rather guttural voice.

So I turn around.

"Slower," he whispers.

So I slow down.

When I have finally completed my turn, he picks me up, peppering kisses on my neck, chin, and chest. He carries me over to the couch, where he sets me down. He gets undressed in a hurried frenzy and kneels before me again.

"Wait," I say. "Let me see you."

CONFIDENT SENSUALITY

He stands, and I gaze at his abs and his beautiful muscled chest. I trail my hands over his body, depositing kisses everywhere. I suck on his nipples, nibbling a bit, feeding off the noises that leave his throat.

My hand trails down to his thick, venous, and curved weapon. I reach for the base and begin sucking on the tip, dropping light kisses in between each suck.

I look up at him, watching his head fall back. I take more of him into my mouth until it hits the back of my throat.

He grabs my head. "Fuck, Melissa."

I moan around his girth, reveling in every second of what I am doing to him.

He pulls me up by my shoulders and whispers, "My turn."

I smirk. "Really?"

He sits me down. "Lay back," he commands.

He pulls my hips toward him and spreads my legs.

I do as I'm told, as he starts depositing kisses on the inside of my thighs. The kisses turn from biting to sucking to licking, and then finally, he gets to my center. I'm already writhing beneath his tongue, so when he gets to my clit, I nearly arch off the damn couch.

Whimpers leave my mouth, and although small, they still leave an echo. I grab his hair, willing him to give me more. I'm starting to climb as he sucks on the tender organ, deepening my arch, adding volume to my echoes.

"Angelo, please."

He groans his approval to my plea against my clit; my breathing sounds like panting. I'm practically screaming, and my writhing is out of control. He grabs my hips to steady me and plunges his tongue inside of me. *That* takes me over the edge. I writhe and scream and convulse until I see stars.

He lets out a short laugh and looms over me. He watches me for a bit before he kisses my lips softly, only teasing me with tastes of myself. He trails said kisses from my lips, then to my cheek, and to my neck. He lingers there, sucking and biting, igniting all my nerves yet again.

I trail my fingers from his forearm to his back to his neck. I grab the hairs that meet with his neck and arch my neck into his lips, silently begging for more. His hand slips between my legs, where he starts to massage my clit.

Fuck. I'm writhing again, thrusting into his fingers, loving every single second of this feeling. His other hands tease my nipple. Sad, pathetic whimpers just keep leaving my mouth without my permission.

But I want more. I want him inside of me.

"Angelo," I say through my heavy breathing. "Please."

He smirks against my neck, "Please what, Melissa?"

"I want you."

"How?"

"Inside of me."

"That's all you had to say."

He pulls back, leaving me cold. He grabs my hips and plunges inside of me. I let out a boisterous cry, filling the cathedral ceilings with my voice.

"Is this what you want?" he asks through gritted teeth.

I nod and whimper because that's all I seem to be able to know how to do. I've lost my words. My senses are speaking for me now.

"Say it," he demands. "Say you want me."

He has my hips in a tight grasp, and he dives into me repeatedly, roughly, quickly. And I'm climbing to my release, until he stops.

"Angelo." His name is a prayer. "Wh—"

He leans down and whispers against my lips, "Say you want me, Melissa."

Well, fuck me. "I want you, Lorenzo." I use his first name because I need him to understand that in this moment, I do not want him. I need him.

And there it is. The animal is born. He begins thrusting deeper and harder but slower. My eyes are rolling, my toes are curling, and those stars have returned.

His arm slips around my waist as he leans down, breathing against my lips. My nails are digging into his back, because I feel this climb preparing to consume me, and he is both my anchor and my iceberg.

He begins kissing me deeply, moaning into my mouth. I call his name through the kissing, but he doesn't stop. He never slows down, so I erupt around him, begging him for something, holding onto him for dear life, and he follows, never ceasing the kiss.

We lay there for what seems like hours. He's plastered against my front. I am barely breathing, but I don't want to move.

What the fuck am I doing?
I'm doomed.

Chapter Fifteen

Lorenzo

What the fuck am I doing?

I am supposed to be planning her demise. Prepping for when her mother comes to find us. Since she is working with my brother, there is only a matter of time before he tells her where I am. Where we are.

My brother wanted to overthrow my father. There has been war between mine and Melissa's family for decades, but Lisa is ruthless. She is relentless. She took my mother away from me. My sister. My father. And she had me watch. I was too young to fight back.

We'd been on vacation. I was only fifteen, my brother was eighteen, and my sister was twenty-one. My brother told her where we were. He told her where to come find us because he was angry that my father did not give him access to the family's tree of wealth upon finally becoming a man. Donatello had always been impulsive, elusive, and selfish. My father was trying to turn him into a man, prepare him for what the future held, but he was not interested. He wanted money, because money to him equates to power.

Lisa offered him a pretty penny to give her our location. She'd been studying our every move. My father knew that Lisa had been studying us, but he trusted us. He trusted his family. We never disclosed our destinations to anyone. That was always understood. He had his own plans, but little did he know, so did Donatello.

Donatello was blinded by his anger and his greed, so he told her everything she needed to know. She knew she could count on him to set his own family up. So she came with Melissa's father. They did what they came to do in front of me. Execution style.

Donatello had conveniently disappeared prior to her arrival. We were not prepared. My father was not prepared to defend his family. She killed them and promised that if I did not decide to join her like my brother, they'd come back for me. I'd like to think that it's because she is uncomfortable with killing minors. That thought would give me the impression that she possesses some semblance of humanity.

I, however, made a deal with her husband, who also fancies money and, conveniently enough, hated her. I wanted intel on her whereabouts so I could have my revenge. He resented her for using their only daughter as leverage to keep him in the game. She would have never hurt Melissa, but he was not convinced due to her ruthless nature. She also loved him, but she loved the game, the power, and the money more. So when she learned of our alliance, she killed him, staging it as self-defense in a domestic violence case. She also killed part of his family when they threatened to report her to Child Protective Services. That is how their cousin, Ramona, came into the picture. Lisa is eccentric.

I retreated after learning of his death, thus losing my source. I took my father's training into consideration. "Patience and silence always yields more information than demands and threats. Take your time, son, and trust no one." I was devoted to studying that family's every move, every falter, and every mistake. This is how I know that Melissa is Lisa's kryptonite.

Their case went cold, and so did my trail. But Melissa, having been five at the time of my family's death, became my new target. It became evident that I'd have to take from Lisa what she took from me. Thus, I was patient, and I was silent. And now, here we are.

The target is in the palm of my hands. Her mother and my brother are no doubt on their way, and I have not begun the final step in this process.

I rise off her chest, and she's fast asleep. Completely vulnerable before me.

"Melissa," I whisper in her ear. "It's time to wake up. I have to show you something."

She moans and mumbles her disapproval.

"Wake up," I repeat another whisper in her ear.

She stirs and begins trailing her fingers up and down my spine absentmindedly. She opens her eyes and leans up to kiss me softly on my lips.

"Five more minutes?"

A laugh involuntarily escapes my throat. "Sure."

I lay next to her on the couch, pulling her back to my front, allowing her to revel in this before everything comes to an abrupt end as she knows it.

*****

I'm awakened to kisses on my neck and jawline. My eyes slowly open to the sight of this beautiful chocolate woman. She took her hair out of its bun, but it does not cascade around her shoulders. Instead, her thick locks float like clouds from another dimension. Her beautiful, plush lips meet mine repeatedly.

"Hello," she greets. "I gave myself a tour of this extravagant cabin.

"Hmph."

"It is just stunning. It's straight out of a Christmas Hallmark movie."

"Hallmark?"

"Oh, that's right. You're old. You don't watch television."

I deposit a genuine laugh in the space surrounding us.

"Can you turn on your back please?"

I oblige, and she straddles me. It's when she sits up that I see she's wearing new lingerie. This one is a sheer bra and, of course, a sheer, crotchless underwear. Her nipples are protruding through the thin material, making every part of me stand on attention.

She leans back down and begins kissing me slowly and sweetly, trailing her hand from my abs to my weapon. She starts rubbing slowly but firmly and whispers "You're so big" against my lips.

Fuck.

Her lips return to mine as she mounts me and puts me inside of her wet and warm entrance. A long, deep moan leans my mouth, making her smile against my lips. She sits up now and begins to ride me, slowly at first. But as her and my climax begin to rise, her hips mover faster. Her screams become louder, and my name comes out of her mouth like she is begging me for more and more and more.

This woman is…going to be the death of me.

We hit our peak at the same time, thrusting into one another, riding the wave of ecstasy all the way home.

She collapses on top of me, breathing heavily, trailing her fingers around my nipple and up and down my chest.

She will be the death of me.

"Come on," I say. "I have something to show you." I sit us up.

"Right now?"

"Yep. Did you buy warm clothes like I told you to?"

"Of course." She smirks at me.

"Then go get dressed. I bought you boots."

She reluctantly gets up, grabs one of the shopping bags out of the foyer, and begins to don her attire: jeans and a sweater.

"Where's your jacket?"

She forms an "oh" with her mouth. "How long will we be out?"

"Long enough for you to need a jacket."

She deflates. "I didn't buy one."

I shake my head. "I have one."

I stand, put my clothes back on, grab her a jacket, and hand her the boots I bought for her.

"Timberlands? These are very nice. Look at you! Knowing fashion!"

I shake my head at her. "Come on. The sun is setting."

She follows me to the back door that leads to a trail, which leads to the Tiasquam River. The trail is beautiful this time of year, with the snow freshly fallen. She and I walk hand in hand down the trail to the river.

I ask her about her childhood, and she tells me about annoying multi-language tutors, additional homework outside of school, her charming cousin, Ramona, and her precious, sweet mother, Lisa.

At one point, her feet begin to hurt, so she checks the size of the boots I bought her. "Lorenzo, these are a nine, I wear a ten."

"Ah, that's right. You have large feet."

She laughs, rolling her eyes at me. "Let's turn around. This charming trail is about to become very uncomfortable."

"We're almost at the river. I'll carry you back."

"Oh? How chivalrous."

I shrug. "I try."

We walk a few more steps, but she stops and says, "Okay, just carry me now because these boots are making my dogs bark."

I laugh as I allow her to mount my back so I can carry her the rest of the way to the river.

Lisa is on her way, so I'll make this quick.

Lisa

My world. My heart and my soul begin to leak out of me in oceans.

I will murder him. I will end his life in a torturous fashion.

My sweet, sweet Melissa.

She's gone.

CONFIDENT SENSUALITY

I'm standing by the river about three miles behind the safe house Donatello told me about. Apparently, Donatello had been bitter since he felt that his father left it to Lorenzo and not him. They have quite a bit of bad blood between the two of them. I thought I could have used all that pent-up bitterness to help me in this absurd plan.

I wanted to kill Lorenzo, and I thought that the best way to draw him to me was through my sweet Melissa. I thought I'd created a masterpiece of a plan. I thought he'd fall in love with her, and then I would use that silly emotion to get him to surrender to her, my Melissa, and then I'd go in for the kill.

But he took her instead.

I wipe the lone tear breaking free.

I should have acted sooner; I should have taken my shot when I had a clear open view. I had ample opportunities. And I did not take them because I had to stick to the plan. In all my years of eradicating human beings, nothing good ever came from straying from the plan.

I shake my head, vigorously wiping the cold tears from my face. "I had everything planned down to a tee," I whispered. "I don't understand."

Now I look back at the trail of footsteps as if they would give me an answer. They started out as two sets of feet and ended with one set. The much larger footprints lead to the river and stops right there.

"Fuck!" I cry out.

I'm not stupid, I've been in this business for a very long time. He likely drugged her, and somewhere during their nice little hike, she succumbed to the drugs, collapsing in the arms she grew to trust. He then carried her the rest of the way to the river, where he disposed of her lifeless body.

Sobs wrack my body. My child is somewhere out there because Lorenzo lured her out here. He made her empty promises, made her feel special, and took her away from me. He did everything I wanted Melissa to do. She was not ready, and I should have known that. Now she is gone.

I look down at my shaking hands, wondering again where I went wrong.

My phone starts to buzz in my pocket. I reach for it, remembering that I told Donatello to call me as soon as he spots his brother.

"Where is he?" I ask.

"Sitting in his living room. He is in plain view."

"I will be there shortly. Keep him in your sight."

"He does not look like he's getting up anytime soon. He's quite immersed in whatever he's working on."

Of course, he is.

Then I ask him, because I am still hopeful. "Do you see her anywhere?"

He hesitates. "No, Lisa."

"Where is Ramona? Has she been able to get in there? We need to have him surrounded."

"She's working on it."

I fight the sobs threatening to rip me apart at the seams. "I am on my way."

Chapter Sixteen

Donatello

I let Lisa in through the back door, which leads to the kitchen. I can tell she wants to look for her precious daughter, but I shake my head, indicating that there's simply no time for that. Knowing my brother, he's already aware that we're here. We need to move quickly.

I do feel badly for the woman, but she had to have known that perhaps placing her only child in the midst of a several-decade-old feud holds little promise of her coming out alive. I just couldn't understand how someone so intelligent could go headfirst into her own death. That someone being Melissa, of course. Regardless, this was poorly planned on Lisa's part.

You never make your weakness disposable. If my father taught me anything, it was that. Do not go around parading your weakness unless you truly do believe you do not have anything to lose. Lisa was trying to be fancy though. She thought that if she paraded Melissa around, Lorenzo wouldn't believe that she is in fact Lisa's weakness. But her downfall is that she forgot that she's a mother before a mafia lord. She boasts and boasts and boasts some more about how profound her kid is. How did she not expect Lorenzo to pick up on that?

He's no walk in the park himself.

I mean look at him. He played it well. He presented Melissa as if she were the love of his life, allowing Lisa to believe that he wouldn't follow through with his initial plan. She wouldn't usually fall for such a thing, but because Melissa is her prized possession, it was easy for her to believe that Lorenzo loves her perfect, stunningly beautiful daughter. I have to tip my hat off to him. He just ended a life and sits there comfortably, probably basking in how beautifully his plan has unfolded.

Our father always favored him, always taught him more of the ropes than he did me. I never understood why. I was older. I was next in line for the throne, the money, and the power. It just seemed like he preferred to give all of that to Lorenzo, so I knew what I had to do. I had to take what was due to me. Sadly, there was little I knew about being up there, so I sought Lisa out. Needless to say, she failed me. I thought she knew better.

We need to get the show on the road. Cleaning up the mess that she's about to make will take quite a while. "Lisa, why don't you take care of the subject in the living room, and I'll search the house for Melissa, yes?"

"Where the fuck is Ramona?" she questions.

"Guarding the front door."

"What the fuck for?"

"She believes Melissa is still alive and will try to escape."

Now Lisa's interest is peaked; she has more motivation. I have to tell her. "You're both a bit too hopeful. Lorenzo is ruthless. Melissa is dead. You need to finish this."

She nods reluctantly. The pain is quite evident in her blue eyes; her daughter took that feature from her father. She sports (or sported) honey-brown eyes. I silently tsk, because it's not like the color of her eyes matter now.

I gesture toward the living room as another silent reminder to Lisa to keep moving. I then make my way up the stairs that are in the kitchen, feigning my interest to search for her child. I continue up the stairs, looking at the pictures that are on the wall of my father, my brother, and me. We are all much younger. I spot my father's button from his favorite peacoat on the last step. He was wearing that jacket when we took him out.

Lisa said she left this at Lorenzo's other house to imply that his death is on the horizon. That's one of her signature moves. She leaves signs around her victims' homes that either they or a loved one will die at her hands. Ironic how I spot this button right after discovering her own child is dead. I nearly laugh. We are truly a sick group of people. I get to the top of the steps and set the button-down on one of the end tables that sits up against the wall outside the bathroom.

The hallway on the second floor is rather long, yet I still manage to spot a moving figure in the bed at the very end of said hall. Ramona is still downstairs; even with that being said, she would never just get in the bed in the home of our enemy.

I see a steady rise and fall of breasts.

"What the fuck?" I whisper.

She stirs again, reaching for something to her left. When she realizes it's not there, she sits up and stares directly in my eyes.

"What the fuck?" She said it this time.

"Lis—"

Bang!

She gasps at the sudden loud and abrupt noise. Recognition settles in, and she flies out of bed. I trail behind her, and as I reach out to grab her, she swings around, gun in hand, with absolutely no tremor in her stance.

She's naked.

And might I just add that in this moment, I am very proud of my little brother.

"Tell me, Donatello." Melissa is very calm. "Do you value your life?" she whispers.

Melissa

Lorenzo was right. The hike we took was breathtaking. I had to stop a few times because the boots he bought me were too damn tight, so halfway to this famous river he wanted me to see, he picked me up. He literally carried me to the river on his back. I am no lightweight, so he is very strong. Of course, I told him as much, and he just chuckled in that way that makes my toes curl.

Except I couldn't curl my toes because the boots wouldn't allow the action.

We made it back to the house, where he promptly removed the boots, smiling up at me, apologizing

CONFIDENT SENSUALITY

for not paying closer attention to my abnormally large feet.

I laughed. "You never seemed to have a problem with my feet, and I think it's because I make up for that in so many ways."

I was sitting at the kitchen bar, watching him open up a bottle of water. "There are plenty of men that won't complain about these feet of mine, Angelo."

He put down the bottle of water that he was trying to drink and charged toward me, like he was the bull and I was the red cape.

I fly off the bar stool and up the stairs, where he tackled me. "What'd you just say?"

My arms were above my head, held firmly in his very strong hands, and he was grinding into me. "Nothing!" I cry out, half laughing, half moaning.

"Don't lie to me." He leans in and bites and nibble on my neck, shooting all sorts of sensations straight to my core. "I'd hate to deny you what's yours."

He unraveled me right on the top of the stairs, then again against the wall, and then again on the largest bed I've ever been on.

Except on the bed, he seemed to have been making love to me. He went slow and whispered torturously sweet words to me. On that bed is where he made me feel like somehow things might be okay. Somehow, I'll graduate college, I'll fix my relationship with my mother, and he and I will start something amazing.

I fell asleep in his arms with hope coursing through my veins.

*****

When I awoke, there was a different feeling surging through my veins, placing my nerves on edge. I roll over, but Lorenzo was gone, and someone else's presence was gaining momentum. I heard distant movement, but I sensed it wasn't him.

I knew it was not Lorenzo.

That feeling that something simply was not right was looming over me, so I sat up, making eye contact with Donatello.

Now, standing before this elusive, mysterious man that seems to turn up at the most unexpected times, I have my gun pointed toward him.

Oddly enough, I do not remember this gun being here prior to my falling asleep.

"Tell me, Donatello. Do you value your life?" I whisper.

He laughs. "I value mine a little more than your boyfriend values his."

I remember the loud noise that startled me into action and the fact that I woke up in bed alone. But if Donatello is up here—

"Donatello!" A voice that I am very familiar with calls his name.

This cannot be happening right now.

I glance at the man on the other side of the gun.

"Move," I say, not even recognizing my own voice.

He follows my command and starts to move toward the steps. I push the gun up against his back as a gentle reminder of who is in charge.

"Donatello, come on. I need a little help," the voice calls again. Something in my psyche refuses to acknowledge who that voice belongs to.

Déjà vu berates me. It mocks me. It is taunting me.

My heart will more than likely shatter my rib cage by the time we make it down the steps.

I don't hear Lorenzo's voice.

I don't fucking hear it.

"Donatello, get down here. I know you hear me!"

We make it to the bottom of the steps that lead to the living room.

And I see it.

The love of my life lies on the floor, bleeding profusely. There is so much blood. Why is there so much blood? He lays beneath my mother's indifferent features. There is still, however, a steady rise and fall of his chest.

My mother holds the gun that may as well have put a bullet through me.

"Mom?"

She startles, drops the gun, and grips her chest.

"Melissa?" She looks confused and lets out this gut-wrenching sob. "Oh my God, you're alive!"

Lorenzo's head turns slowly. An agonizing moan escapes his lips.

My mother begins moving toward me. "Don't," I say, holding up my free hand.

I see her wheels turning. She sees where I'm pointing my gun, and confusion settles into her features once more.

"What are you doing, honey?"

"Do not honey me," I demand.

I glance over at Lorenzo again, taking in all the blood. His lips look pale. He's losing too much blood. "Lorenzo?" I call.

His head turns toward me slowly. "What are you doing?" he asks. "You have to get out of here," he demands. He tries to move but grabs his side in pain.

I look at my mother, who still seems enamored with my appearance.

Ignoring Lorenzo's plea, I ask my mother, "What the fuck is going on?"

"Melissa! Honey, it's me! Your mother!" Her brows furrow.

This woman possesses my mother's face and her figure. However, her mind and her thoughts belong to an evil, manipulative woman that I do not recognize.

"You are a lot of things, but you are not my mother."

She grips her chest again, gathering a significant amount of air to express her shock at my words.

Still putting on a fine performance, I see.

This entire cluster fuck of a situation is all too familiar to the night I lost my father. I remembered thinking, *At least I still have my strong and amazing mother.* As I got older, I always felt like the relationship I had with my mother was gained at the loss of my father. So at the time, I didn't think I lost much, but now that I am meeting my mother for the first time, so many questions arise. All these years, who have I been living with? Who is this woman that raised me?

I ask her the million-dollar question. "You killed him, didn't you?"

"He's clearly not dead," Donatello's random voice shoots in.

"Fuck you," I say, jamming the gun into his back.

I look at my mother once more. "Answer me, Lisa!"

"He was going to kill you!" she says, pointing an accusatory finger in Lorenzo's direction.

"My father," I say, bringing back some semblance of control to my voice. "You killed him." It is not a question.

"You know what happened! You were there!" she cries.

I shake my head, glancing over at the love my life again, fighting the urge to let the sobs rip through me like a tsunami. "No. I do not know what happened."

"Melissa, please." She's crying now.

I have no fucks left to give. "What happened to my father?" My voice is unrecognizable.

"She killed him." Ramona's puny voice makes an unwelcome entrance. "She poisoned him because he did not want to be a part of our family business anymore. He was going to betray us, like you're doing right now."

She walks over to stand next to the woman I once called my mother.

I tilt my head, putting all the puzzle pieces together. "Is that how Ramona's parents died too, Mother?"

Ramona gasps. "Don't you dare!"

"Answer me!" My voice bounces off the walls and the ceilings.

She nods through her sobs. "I severed their brake lines. Their accident was planned. They were going to reveal my operation. They had too much evidence on me."

Ramona doubles over in tears, and Donatello finds his way to her side.

I lower my gun, maintaining eye contact with my mother. "You make me sick. If I live the rest of my life and I never see you again, I'd consider it a life well-lived. Get the fuck out."

She looks hurt, but that quickly transitions to anger. She lunges for the gun on the floor, but Lorenzo grabs it. My mother stills.

"You're just going to allow him to point a gun at your mother?" she wails.

I shake my head. "You're not my mother."

She dives for the gun again.

Bang!

Everything happens within seconds.

Ramona lets out a scream, collapsing in Donatello's arms.

"What did you do?" Donatello shouts.

I lift my gun, pointing it at my mother. "I am not going to say it again. Everyone, get out."

Donatello rushes Ramona out. My mother stares at me for an extra several seconds.

"Now," I demand.

"You will regret this. The both of you." She storms out.

Seconds later, tires are screeching.

I go to Lorenzo's side to examine the source of bleeding. He's been hit in his chest and leg, but the blood is pooling around his left leg. I try to move his pant leg to get a better look at the wound, but he jolts in pain.

Tears break free as I caress his face.

"Lorenzo, stay with me," I plead, pulling his phone from his pocket. There's so much blood.

"I'm here," he answers, revealing his bullet vest.

"Wh—"

"I knew…" He grimaces. "I knew they were coming."

"But you're still hurt, Lorenzo," I say, frantically examining him again.

"Don't worry," he assures me. "I'm fine."

"You are not fine," I say through tears. "We need to get you to the hospital. You can barely move."

"We cannot go to the hospital. They'll ask too many questions," he says through gritted teeth.

"What are we going to do?" Panic is setting in. "You're bleeding a lot." I'm shaking. "Jesus Christ, Lorenzo. We have to do something."

He touches my face, smearing blood on it, I'm sure. "I have a friend who's a doctor. We will call him, and he'll patch me up nicely."

"A friend? What if he doesn't pick up?" I ask, still taking the friend's number. I call, firing all kinds of prayers to the heavens. A calm British accent greets me on the other end of the line.

"This is Dr. Rampasatt."

I tell him where we are and, briefly, what took place.

"I'll be there in a couple of minutes. Please apply pressure to the wound until I arrive," he orders rather politely.

I might be losing my mind, but it almost seemed like he knew he'd be getting that call.

His doctor friend shows up within minutes while I tried to hold pressure on his leg wound.

Dr. Rampasatt is an attractive young Indian man. He's tall with great hair. It's dark and wavy. He has a chiseled jaw and a great smile.

He starts an IV and gives him a sedative, fluids, a blood transfusion, and antibiotics. He then patches his leg up, showing me the entry and exit wound of the bullet, promising that no major arteries were affected. He then gives me a couple of prescriptions to fill: one is a painkiller, and the other is another antibiotic.

"Has this happened before?" I ask. "This all seems a bit routine for you."

Dr. Rampasatt laughs. "Yes. He'll be just fine. He, uh"—he clears his throat—"he actually called me a few hours ago, telling me that he'd need me to free up my schedule for today."

I stare at him. *Of course.*

"Call me," he continues, "if that dressing starts to look red, begins bleeding again, drains pus, or if he develops a fever."

"Okay."

"I will call to check on him tonight."

"Great. Thank you, Doctor."

I see the kind doctor out. He must owe Lorenzo a favor or ten. I swear, every day it is something new with Lorenzo. Today, however, takes the cake.

I go lie next to him and place his head on my chest, whispering promises to not leave his side.

I don't know where my mother and her little gang have disappeared to, but I know that this isn't the end, and I know we cannot stay here for long. I also don't know if my cousin made it as the shot hit her side near a great deal of vulnerable internal organs. Either way, her injury will most certainly buy us some time as I'm sure it has thrown an additional wrench in Lisa's deceptive plan. When Lorenzo awakens, we'll make a plan. Wherever he leads, I will follow.

Chapter Seventeen

Lorenzo

I wrote Melissa a letter just in case things did not go as planned. I wanted her to know what kind of person her mother is. I wanted her to know that I thought the world of her despite how her mother made her feel.

She is a force to be reckoned with. She saunters about in such sensual confidence. She conquered every emotion I tried to weaponize. She never faltered in her steps, and I inevitably fell in love with her. I fought it for a great deal of time, but I began to crave her skin, her lips, her smile, her aura, her light touches, and the scars she left on my back when I became one with her.

She stripped me of my pride; she exposed me to myself. She took all that I am and made me Lorenzo Marcel Angelo.

Lisa was right. I was in way over my head from the beginning. I may have gotten a few physical wounds, but nothing compares to the imprint that Melissa left on my life.

*****

Bella, my love,

You are a woman of unbelievable depths. Your intellectual capacity exceeds many. You have introduced me to myself, and because of that, I owe you a life. I owe you a promising future.

I am sorry that this is how I had to reveal the truth about your mother, but I am not sorry that you have finally met her. I had to plan it this way. You deserve to know, Melissa. But you should also know that you are not defined by your family's mistakes and decisions.

I have fallen for you in ways words cannot express. You are so strong with so much light. I am prepared to love you wholly and completely.

If at the end of this war, you are walking alone, just know the world is yours. Every battle that you stand up against is won because you, my love, are a force of nature.

You are also my everything.
With all my love,
Lorenzo Marcel Angelo

I will not, however, give this letter to Melissa yet. We have more work to do. We have more demons to conquer. There are more skeletons in the closet. They will be back for more. Lisa will beckon her army; my army is right by my side. I drift back off into the realm of sleep, trusting with everything that I am in good hands.

Donatello

Lisa did not bat an eyelash when they told us that Ramona may not make it. They told us that the bullet punctured her left kidney. They told us that the kidney takes up about thirty percent of the heart's blood supply. That means she has already lost an excess amount of blood. They may have to remove the kidney, and because of how much distress her body has already endured, she is not likely to make it. Lisa shed a waterfall's worth of tears for her precious Melissa, but not a single tear fell from her eyes when they told her that she may lose Ramona forever.

"You need to go," I tell her, refusing to make eye contact since she does not deserve that respect.

"Excuse me?" She is beginning to put forth her best theatrics again.

"You heard me."

"Or what?"

"Lisa, stop! Don't fuckin' push me. I may lose the love of my life. I don't like that you're still breathing."

She stares at me, unmoving.

I look at her now, challenging her stance. "You heard me. Get the fuck out." We're nose to nose.

She smirks at me mischievously. "The love of your life," she repeats. "How special."

The doctor interjects, "They are taking her into surgery now."

I step away from Lisa.

"We will do our best to keep you updated," he continues. "However, this procedure will take an immense amount of time. Please take into consideration going home, freshening up, and coming back. I try to suggest that to all my patients' loved ones."

"Thank you, Doctor…"

"Ah, Dr. Rampasatt." He smiles kindly at me, reaching his hand out, offering silent reassurance. His line of vision seems to have slipped beyond my gaze, so I turn around to catch sight of Lisa exiting the emergency room.

Good riddance.

However, this is not the end. A new era has begun. A new level in Lisa's game has begun. She may have lost a few players, but she has not lost her momentum.

I return my gaze to offer my thanks to Dr. Rampasatt again, but I am greeted with his retreating back. He slips his hands in his pockets, sporting quite the chipper demeanor for an emergency surgeon.

*****

I go to the hotel, nap, shower, change, eat, and return to the hospital within five to six hours.

When I get there, I ask a nurse at the nurse's station when Ramona is due to come out of surgery. She clicks a few buttons and says, "Any minute now actually, but she'll be going to a different floor."

She tells me the room number, so I go to that room and await my love's arrival. Seconds feel like hours. Minutes feel like days, then she arrives with tubes entering her body from what seems like every angle.

She is asleep and pale.

Dr. Rampasatt trails behind them, looking through her chart and openly discussing his findings with his colleagues.

He finally meets my eyes and states, "Ramona will recover. She will be sleeping for the majority of the night into the vast majority of the day. This was a rather tolling procedure for her body. Be patient. She is in great hands here. I will be checking in periodically as well."

He shakes my hand again, and of course, I shake his with a bit too much force. He doesn't seem to mind.

"It was my pleasure, Donatello," he says.

I am losing my shit because I don't remember ever introducing myself to Dr. Rampasatt. I must have said my name at some point. It doesn't matter. He saved Ramona's life.

I pull my chair up to Ramona's side, reaching for her hand. "I am not going anywhere."

Dr. Rampasatt

I walk down the hall and stop at the nurse's station. "Hi there. The patient in Room 111 is very fragile. Be sure to pass that along to the night shift nurse."

"Of course, Doctor."

I nod and move along.

"Oh, by the way," she calls, "you have a message from a Mr. Lorenzo. Would you like to return that call?"

"Oh no. Don't worry. I have already spoken with him. Thank you. Take care."

ABOUT THE AUTHOR

Ashley's passions lie in the visual and performing arts. She has expressed her sense of self in paint brushes, pen strokes, her vocals, and her vocation as a nurse. She was born and raised in Brooklyn, New York. When she was in her early teens, her family relocated to Maryland, a place in which she felt offered too little opportunity. So after living in Maryland independently for two years, she relocated to Los Angeles, California. She was educated at Notre Dame of Maryland and is currently pursuing her master's degree in nursing from Walden University.

Since moving to Los Angeles, she has performed in her first musical, *The Cabaret*, took part in her first advertisement shoot for coconut water, curated her first art show, composed her first song, and has now completed her first book. In her words, "It is my hope that many women and men who read this book will find strong connections to the characters."